A Holiday Bet

Giselle Lumas

A Holiday Bet

ISBN: 978-0-9817934-8-1

©2014 Giselle Lumas

Revision © 2024 Giselle Lumas

Donty Books

dontybooks@yahoo.com

Although working hard is often a great trait, it's not so great when you work so much you don't have time for those who love you. Spend time with the ones you love. Every day is not promised.

CHAPTER ONE

"Good morning, everyone," Claire Buchanan greeted her co-workers as she walked into the break room of Robinson Software and Design, where she worked in Palm Hills, California. She let out a yawn as she poured herself a cup of coffee, adding cream and lots of sugar.

"Good morning to you, Trick," Roberta Jenkins said with a snort. "Did you give the mighty strong Carl a treat last night?" She laughed at her own joke. Roberta sat at the small round white table, sipping green tea.

"Ha, ha, ha…" Claire said. "Actually… He gave me three treats last night and one this morning." She grinned wickedly before taking a sip of coffee.

"Really, do you people have to talk about your sex lives on a daily basis?" Sarah Alexander groaned in disgust. "I thought HR was here to prevent this kind of discussion in the workplace, James." Sarah swayed her hips as she made her way to the microwave and paused to glare at James, who was focused on eating his bowl of cereal.

James laughed and said, "Oh, honey, we are on break, which means I'm not HR right now. Anything goes in the break room." He winked. He was sitting at the table with Roberta. Only the four of them were in the room. "So, you may be the VP out there on the floor," James said, pointing to the door leading to the fluorescent-lit gray cubicles of mundane work. "But in here, you are just a regular person like the rest of us."

Sarah groaned again. She unwrapped an enormous blueberry muffin and stuck it in the microwave for a few seconds. She put her red, polished, manicured hands on her slim, narrow waist and narrowed her brown eyes again at James. "I'm pretty sure that company policy applies to the break room as well…"

James pushed up his glasses exaggeratedly with his left middle finger and grumbled, "Don't you have a refrigerator and small microwave in your office?"

"Yes, but I prefer the ones here in the break room," Sarah explained.

"So, what did you do for Halloween last night, Sarah?" Roberta asked, changing the subject.

"I turned out the lights in front of the house and read through a stack of reports in my bedroom," she said. The microwave dinged, and then she carefully retrieved her muffin. Before walking out of the break room, she said, "Personally, Claire, I don't know how you do it. I don't have time for all of that. One-night stands are so much more convenient... no obligation. Do the deed and go home."

James almost choked on the frosted flakes he was chewing on. Roberta laughed. Claire stood with her mouth agape from disbelief.

Finally, Claire shook her brunette head. Her straight waist-length hair flowed side to side as she did so. After a moment, she took another sip of coffee and said, "You know... we really need to do something for Sarah."

Roberta shook her head in disagreement. "Um... don't you mean she should do something for us? We work for her. I think we do enough."

Claire shook her head again, "No... I mean... Sarah is so sad. It's heading towards the holidays. Don't you think she should have someone to love?"

It was James's turn to shake his head, "Nope. She is the type of person that would not appreciate love. She only wants facts and figures. I mean... you just heard the woman. She doesn't want cuddling and softness. Personally, I don't think she has the ability to love."

"Oh, that's a bunch of nonsense, James. Everyone has the ability to love. I've been with this company since its conception thirty years ago. Yes, Sarah is the most rigid of all, but I've seen the soft side of her. I mean, look at what she puts up with from us daily. She could have had all of us fired for one reason or another. Lord knows we aren't the most ethical group at the company."

James laughed.

Claire pointed out, "James is the worst one out of all of us, and he is HR. "

James rolled his dark brown eyes. "Look... HR stands for Human Resources... I'm human and a resource," James said as if that somehow explained everything.

"Yes, you are a resource to scandal, and how to cover it up," Roberta said.

James laughed and raised his right hand up for a high-five. "You got that right."

Roberta slapped his hand.

Claire shook her head. "Guys, really... we need to do something.

Roberta crossed her arms, her well-endowed plump breasts spilled over her arms. "What do you suggest, Claire?"

Claire began pacing the floor. Her shiny black stiletto's click-clacked as she paced back and forth. Her mug of coffee was still in her hand. "Hmmmm..."

"Uh oh..." Roberta elbowed James. "She's really thinking about this."

James raised his eyebrows.

"Well, my brother would probably soften up Sarah."

"Which one?" Roberta asked.

"The only one who lives out here," Claire said. She sat down at the table. She put her elbows on the table and cradled her chin in her right palm. "My other brothers are in Texas. Jeremy is the only one living here in Cali."

"What does he do?" Jeremy asked.

"He's an elementary school teacher in Beach City."

"Hmmm.... The beach will work, but I doubt Sarah will go for a teacher," James said.

"Yeah, I have to agree with James, Claire. Sarah is only into the six- or seven-figure kind of guy. Doctors, lawyers, politicians... you know?"

"But maybe that's the problem. Sarah has been spending most of her time looking for the materialistic stuff or the stuff that looks good on paper, but what she really needs is what fits into her true heart."

"This coming from a woman who has a different boy toy every other week," James said.

"Hey… we aren't talking about me," Claire said defensively. Keep the focus on Sarah."

James glanced at the time on his cell phone. "Well, I have to return to HR mode." He stood and clapped his hands twice to emphasize. "We need to get to work, ladies." James straightened his gray jacket, brushed off his black pants, and adjusted his tie.

Roberta grunted as she rose to her five foot two inches. "You tall people get on my nerves," she said suddenly. "Really Claire, why the heels? You already tower over me in flats."

Claire only stood straighter, "I feel empowered in heels. You should try it sometimes, Roberta."

"Oh, Honey, I've been there and done that in my twenties. When you get to be my age, you go for comfort."

As they walked out the door and entered the world of fluorescent lights and cubicles, Claire said, "I'll call or IM you guys when I'm ready for lunch."

"Okay," James and Roberta said in unison.

A few minutes later, Claire slid into her desk directly in front of Sarah Alexander's office. Being Sarah's personal and administrative assistant was challenging. Roberta and James didn't witness Sarah's mood swings as she had. Claire knew for certain Sarah was lonely. She believed Sarah worked as hard and as long as she did to avoid loneliness.

Jeremy Buchanan was standing in front of the flag pole at Beach City Elementary with the microphone in his hand. The elementary school students and faculty were all gathered around the pole for the morning announcements. He wasn't only the third-grade teacher, but he was also the vice principal as well. Oftentimes, he was the one providing the school with updates and reminders of upcoming events. He was five feet four inches tall, muscular, and wore dress shoes most days. Today was Monday, so he wore gray slacks, black shoes, and a simple white polo shirt. His chest muscles bulged a bit; his biceps were well-defined as he held the mic with one hand and a sheet of paper in the other. He was wearing prescription sunglasses since the sun shone down on him as if it were a spotlight made just for him. "We have three birthdays today. Twins Jessica and Rebecca are from third grade, and Robert is from fifth grade. Are we ready to sing?" Jeremy asked the crowd.

"Yes!" Most of the crowd shouted.

"Okay, on the count of three... one... two... three..." Jeremy led enthusiastically. Everyone began singing Happy Birthday.

When the singing was over, Jeremy announced. "Okay, everyone, that's the announcements for the day. Choose to have a great day. You only have a bad one if you make it one."

The teachers, along with their aides, shuffled their students to their respective classrooms.

As Jeremy walked his class, one of the student's mothers walked alongside him. "Hi, Mr. Buchanan. I wondered if we could meet after school to discuss my daughter."

"Oh, sure, anytime. Who is your daughter?" Jeremy asked. He stopped before his classroom, gesturing for the kids to go inside. Jeremy stood next to the doorway and turned to look at the mother for the first time. She was an inch shorter than he was. The woman was slim, with brunette curly hair pulled back into a stylish ponytail. She wore jeans and a tight-fitting magenta T-shirt. He tried not to appreciate her figure; it was a challenge, but nonetheless, he succeeded.

"I'm Leslie Jenkins. Lori Jenkins is your student."

He smiled when he noticed the resemblance between mother and daughter. He glanced inside the classroom and saw that Lori just happened to be wearing jeans and curly brunette hair like her mom. "I can see that." He crossed his arms and looked into her brown eyes. "What did you need to talk to me about?"

"Well, her father and I are getting a divorce, and I just want to talk about the best way to keep Lori's grades on track and ensure her father doesn't pick her up. He doesn't have custody right now. I just... we... I would like to discuss further later today if you don't mind."

He uncrossed his arms, took a deep breath, and nodded in agreement. "Of course. I understand. Divorce and custody battles can take a toll on the kids. Yes, we can meet. Would three o'clock later today work?"

Leslie gently placed a slim, manicured hand on his right bicep. "Oh, thank you. I truly appreciate it."

"No problem. I will see you later," Jeremy said.

She removed her hand and turned to leave. Jeremy did his best not to stare at her rear end as she walked away. He entered his classroom and closed the door. "Okay, class, let's get started." He clapped his hands once and stood front and center in the class.

Around eleven o'clock, Sarah summoned Claire into her office. Clair sat across from her boss with a notepad and pen. Claire studied Sarah for a few minutes as she waited for her to wrap up an email she was sending. Sarah tended to wear her chestnut brown hair slicked back into a French twist on a daily basis. Claire wondered if she ever wore her hair down during the weekends. Claire also wondered if Sarah even had weekends. What did she do on the weekends? Sarah obviously worked out. She was slim but curvy. She had a narrow waist to die for. Claire knew all of her brothers would appreciate Sarah's backside and breasts. Sarah's breasts were probably a borderline B/C. Was it appropriate to be wondering what size breast your boss was? Claire shifted in her seat. She was only thinking of her brothers. It was appropriate.

"What's your preference in men?" Claire asked without thinking. Sarah was still typing her email but stopped in shock to stare at Claire.

"Excuse me?" Sarah asked.

"What's your preference for men? Do you have to have a man who earns six, seven, or eight figures annually? Does it matter? Does height matter? Does nationality or ethnicity matter?"

Sarah frowned and tilted her head, "Um, Claire, don't you think that is a little personal?"

"Well, you hired me as your administrative and personal assistant. So assisting your personal life's also part of my job."

Sarah blinked.

"Sarah?" Claire asked.

"Yes?" Sarah asked.

"So... tell me..."

Sarah cleared her throat. "Not that it really is any of your concern, but the amount of money a man makes doesn't matter to me. I make my own. Height though... I'd prefer for him to be taller than me. I've been self-conscious about my height all my life. I was always made to feel like an Amazon alien because I've always been tall."

"How tall are you anyway?" Claire asked.

"Five ten."

"Hmmm...." Claire thought. Her mouth tweaked to the right side of her mouth. "If the man treated you like a queen, would you overlook the height?"

"I don't know, Claire..." Sarah admitted. Exasperated by the conversation, she waved her hand dismissively. "Let me wrap up this email, and then we can get back to work."

"Fine," Claire said with a pout. She continued to think of her brother, Jeremy. Then Claire realized Sarah hadn't answered the other question. "What about nationality or ethnicity? You didn't answer that one.

"Oh, good grief, Claire! I'm Creole. I am probably mixed with every nationality or ethnicity known to the human race… it doesn't matter…. Okay? And no, I will not go on any blind dates ever, so stop plotting now!"

Dejected, Claire slouched in her seat. "Fine," she said in a low voice.

CHAPTER TWO

James drove Roberta and Claire to a food court at a nearby shopping mall at lunchtime. Claire was sitting in the back seat of James' red Mustang convertible. "She asked me to take charge of the Thanksgiving Day Benefit again this year. I am always in charge of the benefit," Claire whined.

"That's because you are so good at it," Roberta said. "No one is more organized than you are, Claire."

"Yes, but someone else needs to do it this year. I planned on going to Texas to be with my parents and other brothers for Thanksgiving this year."

"Well, do you know who else can do it?" Roberta asked.

James parked the car, and then they all got out. Claire frowned and mumbled under her breath, "Why can't one of you?"

Roberta stopped in her tracks and stared up at Claire." Did I just hear you right? Do you want James or me to run the benefit?"

Claire took a deep breath in and then slowly let it out. "Well... yes."

James immediately countered with, "Well... um.... No. Heck to the no!" James shook his head adamantly. "I am not built to be in charge of any form of benefit anything."

"Really?" Claire asked. "You are supposed to be human resources, James! You deal with benefits every day! If you ask me, I think HR should be in charge of this whole annual thing anyway."

Roberta silently resumed walking towards the food court. She stood in line at a taco stand while James and Claire went to a Chinese food stand. Claire and James continued arguing while they were placing their orders. When they had their food trays, Claire said, "Well, James, that is an excellent idea! I accept your challenge."

"Oh shi... shh... shoot," James said with disbelief and frustration evident in his voice.

Roberta was already sitting at one of the concrete round tables in the middle of the mall's courtyard. She gestured for the two of them to sit at the table. "What are you two talking about?"

"Well, the brilliant James here has challenged me to a bet."

Roberta blinked, pursed her lips, and said, "Why do I feel I'm somehow a part of this bet?"

Claire smiled, her sparkling, perfect white teeth gleaming with dimples, then announced, " If I get my brother and Sarah Alexander to go on a date before the Tuesday before Thanksgiving, you two have to cover the benefit, and I get to fly out to Texas."

"What's in it for me?" Roberta asked.

"A happy boss," Claire said.

Roberta rolled her eyes.

"Look, it's not fair that I'm always expected to turn down Thanksgiving Day invitations yearly. I wouldn't mind doing it… in fact, I enjoy doing it most of the time. But I miss my parents, brothers, and my Aunt Judy. She is going to be there. I want Thanksgiving with my family this year, okay?"

James slumped his shoulders as he jabbed his orange chicken with a fork. He looked at Roberta.

"Well…" Roberta thought for a moment. "Fine. It's a fair deal. Maybe I will help out even if you lose… maybe."

There was a sudden spark in Claire's eyes, and she grinned again. "Thanks, Roberta."

"Pssst... I'm telling you now. If you lose, you are washing my car, buying me lunch for a week, AND taking care of the benefit... Putting me through this stress..."

When Claire returned from lunch, she found Sarah sitting at her desk with a scowl on her face. She tried to quietly return to her desk unnoticed, but as she sat down, her chair made a squeaking sound. She quietly cursed the chair. "Claire! Are you back? Come in here, please."

Claire groaned, grabbed a notepad and pen, then entered Sarah's chamber. "Do you know who prepared the contract with Grover's Law Offices? They informed me we agreed to free repairs for an additional year. I reviewed it just now, and yes... we did. Why? Who would do that? I would never sign off on that!"

"Don't you need to contact the legal department to find that out? I mean, the clients themselves are lawyers."

Sarah's hands deformed into claws. "That's not the point. You usually know who is working on what contract, and I thought it would be easier to go to you. Oh... ugh." Sarah abruptly placed her elbows on the table and squeezed her head with her hands.

Claire's face contorted. She would have thought that applying too much pressure to her own head would cause it to explode. She slowly attempted to back out without Sarah noticing.

"Get Legal on the phone! I need to figure this out!"

"Okay," Claire said, then returned to her desk. The rest of the day was consumed with tracking down people Sarah needed to speak to immediately and setting up urgent meetings. Claire's head was throbbing from witnessing Sarah in action. Did the woman ever smile? She couldn't remember.

At the end of the day, she walked out to the parking lot with Roberta and James. "So, have you come up with a plan for getting your brother to date Sarah?" Roberta asked.

"All I need is for the two of them to meet. I'm almost sure of it," Claire said with fake confidence.

"I'm telling you. If your brother isn't a millionaire, he has no chance with Sarah," James said.

"Well, my brothers in Texas are wealthy, but Jeremy isn't. He isn't materialistic."

"Don't you think it's a waste of time then?" James asked.

I think she should try." Roberta said, shrugging her shoulders. "I' don't think Sarah is as superficial as you make her out to be."

"Thank you, Roberta," Claire said. She clicked a button on her key chain. Her Honda Accord beeped twice.

James stood next to his Mustang and appeared a bit worried. "So what's your plan?"

Claire grinned. "They will meet each other tomorrow."

Jeremy was sitting at his desk after school, grading papers. He could have taken his work home but tried his best to avoid it. His cell phone rang. He glanced at caller ID and saw that it was his sister. "Hey, Claire," he answered with a smile.

"Hi Jeremy, what are you doing?"

"Grading papers. What's up?" He leaned back in his chair and stared up at the holes in the classroom ceiling.

"Are you planning to go to Texas for Thanksgiving this year?" Claire asked.

"I was thinking about it, why?

Me too... I was just curious. Hey... um..., would you ever consider going out with a woman who was a lot taller than you?

"Depends... how tall? And how does she look? What's her story?"

"I'm just asking... she would be five-ten." Claire avoided the other questions.

Jeremy shook his head with a grin. He knew his sister well. She never asked a question just for the sake of asking. She was scheming. He could practically hear her brain at work. "That's kind of tall for me. I'd need a ladder just to his her."

Claire laughed. "What if she's beautiful?

I'd consider it," he said honestly. "It's the attitude that has to be beautiful too, though."

Oh," Claire said in a whisper.

He shook his head. "I don't do blind dates, sis. You know that. So stop the scheming now.

"Well, Claire coughed. "What about if you met her before going on a date? Would that work?"

"Depends... I'm not interested in starting a relationship right now, Claire. Just... please... stop the scheme now." He warned her seriously.

"Ah, man..." she groaned. "Well, I have to get ready for a date with Carl. I'll talk to you later. Love you."

"I love you too, sis," Jeremy said. He pressed the end button on his cell phone and shook his head. He tried to mentally brace himself. He knew his sister would not give up. His guess was she would contact him at some point during this week and somehow manage to get him to meet the mystery woman she was trying to set him up with.

CHAPTER THREE

It was Wednesday; Claire had less than three weeks to get her boss and brother to date. She was sitting at her desk creating a spreadsheet per Sarah's request when Sarah asked her to come into her office. Claire took her usual seat in front of Sarah and studied her boss for a few minutes. Sarah was in a gray suit with a white rayon dress shirt. She wore simple gold studded earrings and moderate makeup, which gave a natural look but enhanced her caramel complexion, long lashes, and full lips. Claire assumed she was wearing lip gloss. Jeremy would fall for her. She was certain of it.

"Have you ever been married?" Claire asked, flicking her black pen back and forth and tapping on her small notepad.

Sarah stopped typing and stared at Claire. "Excuse me?"

"You heard my question..." Claire sighed. "Have you ever been married?"

Sarah blinked, cleared her throat, and then said, "Yes, as a matter of fact. I was very young. We divorced after only three months."

Claire's mouth dropped open from shock. She thought Sarah was incapable of making mistakes. Marrying the wrong person at a young age could be classified as a mistake, right?

"You can close your mouth now, Claire. As I said, I was young." Sarah resumed typing out the email she was working on. "I'd also appreciate it if you didn't address me in that tone anymore."

"So, have you had any serious relationships since?"

"I don't have time for serious relationships. I've been building my career and am trying to keep it. I don't have time for nonsense," Sarah said with a wave of her hand.

"Love isn't nonsense," Claire said, thinking of Carl with a sigh. She had to admit to herself that she was falling hard for Carl.

Sarah shook her head. "Why the sudden interest in my personal life? You've been my assistant for over five years now. Why the sudden inquisition?"

"Maybe because I haven't seen you smile for the past five years.

Sarah frowned.

"See…" Claire said, pointing her pen at her boss. "Look at yourself in the mirror right now. That expression right there is the one you normally wear… or you have your elbows on your desk and squeeze your head super hard. One day, I will have to call 911 because you are going to explode. You need to have some fun."

Sarah glanced at a small round mirror she kept near her computer. She tilted her head to the side. "So, you've made it your mission to put love and fun into my life?" She narrowed her eyes and glanced at Claire.

"As a matter of fact, yes," Claire said confidently. She made an effort to sit up straighter in her seat.

"Please stop," Sarah said. "I am delighted with how things are in my life."

Claire squinted her eyes at Sarah but didn't say anything further.

"Now, let's get to work," Sarah said, changing the subject.

During lunch, it was decided to eat in the company's cafeteria. James, Roberta, and Claire were sitting outside on the patio. It was a sunny, clear day in Palm Hills, California. Claire leaned back in the plastic chair, stretched out her arms, and momentarily closed her eyes, soaking in the sun. She smiled.

"So any update on Operation Set Up? James asked before he bit into a French fry.

"Baby steps, James... Baby steps." Claire dipped one of her taquitos into a pile of guacamole and took a bite. She moaned from the satisfied taste.

"Well, you have less than three weeks, Claire" You might need a little bit more than baby steps," Roberta said with a warning. She played with her soggy grilled cheese sandwich, eating little.

"Hey, I thought you were on my side..." Claire whined, glancing at Roberta.

"I'm on my side," Roberta clarified. She shook her head. "I've got enough to deal with at home. I don't need drama here at work."

James asked, "What's going on at home?"

Roberta sighed. "My daughter and granddaughter moved in last night. She's divorcing her no-good husband." She shook her head. "At least the court granted her full custody... for now. He's appealing, of course."

"Oh, I'm sorry," Claire said, gently placing a hand on her friend's arm.

"Oh, it's all going to be okay. I'm glad she finally left him," Roberta said. She shook her head and refocused the conversation. "So, what's your plan?" Roberta asked Claire.

Claire grinned, then said, "They will meet today."

"Humph," James huffed, crossing his arms.

"Uh oh… I've seen that look in Claire's eyes before, James. Don't make any plans for Thanksgiving." Roberta said with a small laugh.

"Humph…" James puffed again.

At four o'clock, at the end of Claire's work shift, she grabbed her little black designer purse and a letter opener. She wandered out to the parking lot and approached her car. Claire glanced around to see if anyone was close by. When she saw that the coast was clear, she made the sign of the cross and said a small prayer of forgiveness for what she was about to do. Claire stabbed the letter opener into the front passenger tire. Her heart was racing, and she knew her face was flush. You would think Claire was vandalizing someone else's car and not her own. She heard the fizz as air leaked its way out of the tire. She rushed back into the building. The security officer squinted his eyes at her. She wondered if he had witnessed the whole thing on video.

She rushed back to her desk, shoved the letter opener back into her desk drawer, and said loudly, "I can't believe it! I just can't... what am I going to do?" She paced dramatically back and forth in front of Sarah's office, the door to which was open. Sarah glanced up and frowned.

"Someone popped my tire!" Claire said with an exaggerated whine.

"What? Why would someone do that?" Sarah asked. She slid from her desk chair and left her office to join Sarah. "Do you want me to call security? They probably have the whole thing on video."

Claire's eyes widened, but she shook her head. "Oh, no. I will call my brother. He'll know what to do."

"Your bother?"

"Yes."

"Okay," Sarah said. Well, let me know if you need anything." Sarah turned back to her office and resumed sitting at her desk, typing on her computer.

Claire sighed in relief and pulled her cell phone out of her purse. She punched in her brother's number. On the third ring, he answered. "Hey Claire, what's up?"

"Um… Jeremy, someone popped my tire. Do you think you can come by my job and change the tire? Please…"

Jeremy immediately felt suspicious and alert. "Don't you have the auto club membership? They can change the tire at no extra charge."

Claire stomped her heeled stiletto foot, then thought quickly and lied, "Oh, no… it canceled. I haven't had a chance to renew the membership." She did her best to sound stressed.

Jeremy knew Claire was the most organized member of his family. She was never late for bills and was in the habit of paying them early. "What are you up to, Claire?" he asked.

"Noth… nothing… please Jeremy. I need your help. You're the only brother who lives close to me… please…" she begged.

He let out a sigh, "Fine; I will be there in twenty minutes." Then, he disconnected the call.

Claire pumped her fist in the air from victory.

"Everything okay, Claire?" Sarah called out from her office

"Oh… yes. My brother will be here in twenty minutes.

"Oh… okay," Sarah said. "Mind typing up a memo while you wait?"

Claire groaned but said, "Okay."

Jeremy called his sister from the parking lot twenty minutes later to inform her he was there. Claire said she would send out her boss to give him the keys to her car. She made up an excuse about needing to go to the bathroom. Jeremy stood beside his sister's car with his hands on his hips, shaking his head. Less than five minutes later, a tall, leggy woman with a caramel complexion and chestnut brown hair pulled back into a tight bun approached him. She had a scowl and appeared rigid in her gray business suit. But he paused for a moment for his eyes to linger on her full lips. *Kissable*, he noted. She was holding Claire's keys in her right hand. "Hi," the woman said. "You must be Jeremy?" She stopped before him, holding the keys out with her index finger.

"Yes, you must be the boss," he smiled, looking up at her. She didn't smile back. *Ouch.*

She nodded and crossed her arms. "Your sister has been behaving quite strangely lately. Is everything okay?"

"Well, nothing is wrong as far as I know... other than this tire."

"Why didn't she call the auto club?" Sarah asked.

"That's what I asked," Jeremy said.

"Well, guess I should change this tire so we can all go home, right?"

"Right," Sarah said, nodding her head. It was nice to meet you." She didn't wait for his response but retreated to the building instead.

Claire met Jeremy in the parking lot fifteen minutes later. "Hi Jeremy, sorry for taking so long. Thanks for coming out." He was almost done tightening the bolts on the spare tire.

"You know, it kind of looks like a letter opener might have been the cause for the slashed tire," Jeremy said suspiciously.

"Oh, what? Really?"

"Were you trying to set me up with your rigid boss?" Jeremy asked as he continued to tighten the bolts.

Claire's eyes widened, and she shook her head vigorously in denial. "Oh, no... of course not. Why would I do that?"

"Who knows..." Jeremy said. "I also remembered Dad teaching you how to change the tire and oil long ago."

"But come on, Jeremy, look at me," Claire said seriously. She used her manicured hands and moved them up and down the white mini-dress she wore.

Jeremy smirked. "Uh, huh... well... look at me." He mimicked her hand gestures to himself. He was in black dress slacks and a white polo shirt.

"But, you're a guy!" She said as if that explained everything.

He shook his head. When he was done, he stood up and looked at his sister. He stared into her eyes. "No more scheming, sis. We are both too old for this nonsense. I don't want to be set up. I especially do not want to be set up with a woman who is rigid and doesn't know how to smile."

"But..." Claire started, pouting.

"No buts. This is it. Okay?"

Claire frowned. "Fine."

CHAPTER FOUR

On Friday, Sarah was predictably in her office typing yet another email when her cell phone vibrated. She glanced at the caller ID and saw that it was her sister-in-law. Her sister-in-law rarely called her during business hours and during her workweek schedule. So she knew it had to be something important. "Hi Kim, everything okay?" she asked after placing the call on speaker so that she could continue typing.

"I'm stuck in traffic, and it looks like I won't be able to get back for at least a couple of hours or so. Can you please pick up the twins from school and watch them until I get to your house?"

Sarah stopped typing from the surprise. "Um... I ... what school do they go to?"

"Beach City Elementary. It should take thirty minutes from your office to get there. If you leave in about ten minutes. I know you are busy, but I don't have any other options... please."

"You know, I live in Beach City, too, so I know how long it takes," Sarah said snappishly.

"Right. I forget that you only live a couple of blocks away from us since we rarely see you, Kim retaliated.

"Um... I..." Sarah had not spent much time with her nieces except for family obligation events. She wasn't sure what to do with them while they waited for Kim to pick them up.

"Sarah, please pick them up. I don't know what else to do. Please... Your brother is in Vegas for a convention. I just had a meeting in Fresno. The twins spent the night at my neighbors' house last night, and then they took them to school... I wouldn't ask you unless I really needed you right now. Besides, you should spend more time with your God children, you know?"

The Catholic guilt immediately slipped into her soul. She let out a sigh. "Okay, fine. Yes. I will pick them up. Do I have to go to the school's office, or what must I do?"

"Yes, you can go to the office and tell them who you are. Bring your ID. You are on the emergency contact list, so you should not have a problem."

"Okay, what time do they get out?" Sarah asked.

"Two thirty," Kim said.

Sarah glanced at the clock on her desk. It was almost two o'clock now. She'd have to basically leave right after she disconnected with Kim. "Okay, I will pick them up and see you at my place."

"Thank you so, so much. I will call the school and let them know. I owe you," Kim said, then disconnected the call.

"Claire!" Sarah called out from her office as she shut down her laptop and started shoving files into her black leather carrying case. "Claire," she called out one more time.

Claire appeared with her hair in a slicked-back ponytail, hooped earrings, a black jumper, and a notepad and pen.

"Surprise! You can go home early today if you've done all you need to do for the day. I have to pick up my nieces."

Claire's eyes widened, "What?" This was the first time ever that Sarah had allowed her to go home early.

"I know... it's a rare thing... but seriously, if you've done all you need to do today, you can go home. I'll finish up later tonight from home."

"Wow! Thank you," Claire said with an enormous smile. Then, she rushed back to her desk to grab her purse before her boss changed her mind.

At Beach City Elementary School, Jeremy was on carpool duty: ensuring students left with whom they were supposed to go home, monitoring parking lot etiquette, and protecting their safety and well-being. There were arrows clearly marked in the parking lot to show the flow of one-way traffic, meaning one way in and one way out. He was watching a couple of kids board the school bus when he heard yelling. He moved away from the bus to witness a silver Mercedes enter the lot from the wrong direction, which wreaked havoc on many parents and students. He massaged the back of his neck and signaled the car to back up and go around to the other side of the street. Jeremy could not see the driver's face because of the sun's reflection on the windshield. A couple of cars tooted their horns, and he could hear a few colorful curse words coming from other drivers. The driver of the Mercedes finally caught on and backed out of the parking lot into the street, then drove around to the entrance part of the lot... All was well.

Or so he thought until a couple of single moms approached him. "Hi, Mr. Buchanan. How are you?"

I will be great when I get home to my condo with a beer in my hand and watch some football. Jeremy wanted to say but instead said, "I'm good. How are you, ladies?"

"Oh, well, we were just talking, and Sheila here thinks she should give you her number so the two of you could go out. But, I was saying that was a bad idea since I really think you and I should gout... at least once... twice... or more."

Jeremy placed his hands on his hips and cleared his throat. "Sorry, ladies, but we have a policy here at the school... no dating students' parents." Of course, he entirely made that up, but they didn't need to know that.

Both women narrowed their eyes. "Hmmm... too bad. Well, if anything changes, here's both of our numbers, " one of them said and handed him a small piece of yellow notebook paper with their names and phone numbers scribbled on it.

He smacked his lips, closed his eyes, and patiently and politely accepted the slip of paper, which he planned to toss into the trash as soon as possible.

"Have a good rest of the day, Mr. Buchanan," one of the ladies said as they waved and walked away.

Jeremy shook his head. He glanced around the parking lot. The afterschool traffic died down quite a bit. He noticed the twins from his class still lingered in the parking lot. They both had a caramel complexion with brunette hair pulled back into a ponytail. One had a blue backpack, while the other had a pink one. Both were in blue jeans and red sweatshirts. "Rebecca, Jessica... why don't you come into the office until your mom or dad arrives?"

The two third graders followed him to the school's office. When they entered the office, a tall woman who looked vaguely familiar was speaking to the school's receptionist. The lady resembled the twins, except her hair was lighter, more of a chestnut brown color. Her hair was slicked back into a tight bun, though, so he didn't know if it was curly or not. She was leaning against the desk with her palms spread out. The woman was obviously upset and meant business. She was wearing a black miniskirt with black tights and black high heels. She wore a white Rayon long-sleeve button-up shirt. Pearl earrings in her ears. A thick gold bracelet on her left wrist. Her attire screamed HIGH MAINTAINANCE. But, boy, was she a knockout!

"Aunt Sarah?" Rebecca and Jessica asked in unison.

Sarah turned from the receptionist and stood straight to face the girls.

Geez! Can she be any taller? Jeremy groaned.

"See, I told you. I'm their aunt," Sarah said to the receptionist.

"And I didn't say I didn't believe you. I only said we needed to wait for Mr. Buchanan."

"Buchanan?" Sarah tilted her head. Recognition illuminated her face. A smile spread across her lips and immediately reached her eyes. Jeremy felt his heart flutter. *What the heck was that? My heart doesn't flutter!* He scowled, annoyed by the unexpected sensation. *Damn! She's beautiful!* He tried to shake off the rush of hormones. He didn't need this.

Sarah pointed to him. "You're Claire Buchanan's brother, right? We met earlier this week, remember? You changed her tire. I delivered her keys."

"Oh, right... I knew you looked familiar. You really should smile more often," Jeremy said without thinking.

She tilted her head, blinked, and licked her lips. Long, thick eyelashes flitted over her beautiful dark brown eyes. His eyes were transfixed on Sarah's full lips. He felt hypnotized and mesmerized.

"Are you picking us up today, Aunt Sarah?" Jessica, the one with the pink backpack, asked.

"Yes, Rebecca, I am," Sarah answered, overly confident.

Jessica scowled. "I'm Jessica." Then, she pointed to her sister. "She's Rebecca."

Sarah's shoulders sagged slightly, but she cleared her throat and smiled tightly. "Oh, well, it's been a while. You know you two are identical, right?'

The receptionist explained to Jeremy, "Mr. Buchanan, I've already checked Miss Alexander's ID, and she is on the emergency contact list. Also, Rebecca and Jessica's mom called to say Miss Alexander will pick them up today."

"Okay, it looks like you are clear to go."

Sarah let out a heavy sigh. She suddenly appeared to be nervous.

"So, girls, don't forget your spelling and vocab homework... oh, and your math worksheet. They are all due Monday."

Sarah frowned. "Who would assign homework on a Friday?"

"Oh, that would be me. Their teacher and vice principal," Jeremy said matter-of-factly. He stood straighter, tilting his head to look up at her.

"Um... oh... well, ready to go, girls? Your mom will be picking you up later from my house."

"Really? Yay! We get to spend time with you!" the one with the blue backpack said. So, the blue backpack twin was more talkative, while the pink twin was more reserved. She'd get their names right before their mom picked them up. It was her mission. Suddenly, Sarah started to feel giddiness inside of her, but there was still an enormous amount of queasiness and uneasiness. What was she supposed to do with two third graders? How old were they anyway?

As they were walking to the parking lot, each of them holding Sarah's hand, Sarah asked, "So, how old are you two"

"Eight," they both answered.

"Huh? When did that happen?" Sarah asked, surprised. "In two years, you will be in the double digits... Geesh!"

"That's what dad says. He says once we hit the double digits, everything just falls apart," Blue Pack said.

Sarah laughed, then said," Our dad used to say that." They stopped in front of a silver Mercedes, and then Sarah let go of their hands. She pressed on her key chain, and the alarm beeped twice. "Well, get in, girls. Who wants to sit in the front?"

"Oh," Pink Backpack said as she shook her head adamantly. "No! Your car has airbags, right?"

"Yes, of course," Sarah said, looking down at the girls.

"Well, we aren't allowed to sit in the front seat until we are twelve. It's the law," Pink Backpack said.

"Jessica, why do you always have to go by the rules? I could have sat in the front. Why don't you keep your mouth shut? Dang!" Rebecca said.

Okay, got it. Jessica is pink and reserved, while Rebecca is blue and the rebel. Hmmm... Rebecca has a tiny mole near her left eye. "Rebecca, apologize to your sister. Never, ever tell her to be quiet. Got it?" Sarah said, squinting her eyes at Rebecca. Then she turned to look down at Jessica, her face softened. "Thank you for letting me know that. I personally don't want to break any laws, nor do I want to ever risk either of your lives. Always speak up and let your voice be heard. Okay?"

Jessica took a deep breath from what appeared to be relief, then smiled a little. "Okay," she whispered.

An hour and a half later, the girls finished their homework. They were both seated at Sarah's oak kitchen table. "Aunt Sarah," Jessica said quietly as she shoved her books and folders back into her backpack.

"Yes?" Sarah asked. She was sitting on the sofa in the living room, going through some reports for work. She had changed into shorts and a USC T-shirt. Even though it was November, it was in the eighties in Southern California.

"I'm hungry."

"Oh," Sarah blinked. *Right... I should probably feed them,* she thought guiltily. "Well, I haven't done much grocery shopping. Why don't I order a pizza for all of us? Your mom can eat some when she gets here."

"Alright!" Both Rebecca and Jessica shouted, then high-fived each other.

For a brief moment, Sarah wondered if her nieces had just played her in some way. "Do you prefer where we get the pizza or what's on it?"

"Pepperoni and sausage, please," Rebecca answered for the both of them.

"Is that what you want too, Jessica?"

"Yes, please," Jessica said with a smile.

Sarah felt her heart begin to swell with love. She really needed to spend more time with them. They were growing so fast. And you both don't care where I order it from?"

"Nope," Rebecca said.

Sarah glanced at Jessica for confirmation.

"Nope," Jessica said.

"Okay. Pizza coming up," Sarah said as she searched for the nearest pizza place that delivers. She found Paul's Italian Pizzeria and placed their order.

The girls watched the Disney channel while they waited for the pizza. Thirty minutes later, the pizza arrived. As Sarah placed the pizza boxes on the granite kitchen countertop, her cell phone rang.

She saw that it was her sister-in-law. "Hi, Kim," Sarah greeted before taking a bite out of a slice.

"Hi, Sarah... um... would you be able to do a huge favor for your favorite brother and me?" Kim asked, sounding suspicious.

"He's the only sibling I have."

Kim cleared her throat. "Look, things have been rough for both of us. Your brother just called me and asked if I could meet him in Vegas for the weekend. We really need some quality alone time together without the girls."

Sarah felt her stomach begin to squeeze. Not sure she liked what was coming next.

"Would you mind watching the girls this weekend? We would pick them up on Sunday night."

"But... you said you were picking them up today," Sarah said, dropping the pizza slice on the paper plate.

The girls stopped eating as well and stared up at Sarah with wide eyes.

"What am I supposed to do with them for a whole weekend?"

"Get to know them," Kim said.

"But..."

"Please, Sarah... I rarely ask for favors. I know you're a busy woman, too, but please... your brother and I really need this. Please...", " Kim begged.

Sarah could hear the rare desperation in her sister-in-law's voice. "Okay, what about their clothes and toothbrushes... hair?"

"You still have a key to our house, right?"

"Yes, I suppose I can take them over there to pick up some clothes and other necessities."

"Thank you so much, Sarah," Kim said, then disconnected.

Sarah had her left hand on her hip while her right hand still held her cell phone. She stared at the phone for what felt like hours but in reality, was only a few seconds.

"Aunt Sarah?" Rebecca asked worriedly. "What's going on?"

Sarah cleared her throat. "Well, you two will be spending the weekend with me. I'll take you over to your house after we eat to pick up a few things."

Jessica and Rebecca stared at each other. Each of them raised their eyebrows questioningly.

CHAPTER FIVE

At six o'clock on the dot, Sarah's eyes fluttered open. She rarely needed to set an alarm because her body automatically woke up at that time, no matter how late she may have stayed up the previous day. She stared at the ceiling and immediately began mentally creating a list of what she needed to accomplish for the day. She paused when she remembered her nieces were staying with her until the following evening. She thunked her forehead with her right hand. *What in the world am I supposed to do with two eight-year-old girls?*

She supposed she should go into the guest bedroom and check on them. Her two-story condo was a nice size for a single woman. She had two bedrooms and two bathrooms upstairs, while the living room, kitchen, half bath, and dining room were downstairs.

Sarah rose from her bed. She was wearing simple, lightweight pajama pants with a matching short-sleeved top. She dragged her feet as she approached her bedroom door. Sarah reached for her blue fuzzy robe that was hanging from a hook on the back of the door. After putting the robe on, she tied it tight around her. Sarah turned the knob and looked at the door directly across from hers. The door was still closed; she quietly turned the knob and took a peek inside.

Rebecca had taken out her ponytail, and her hair was spread out every which way in a tangled mass across her pillow. Rebecca's mouth was wide open, and she was spread out across the queen-sized bed like a starfish; hardly any covers were on her.

Jessica, on the other hand, still had her hair in a ponytail, which was, in fact, now braided and still neat. She was wrapped up tight in a comforter as if in a cocoon and curled in a tiny ball on the edge of the left side of the bed.

Sarah had to cover her mouth to hold in her laughter. What a sight her nieces were! She would love to have taken a picture of them now but didn't want to risk waking them. It was funny how they looked so much alike but had completely different personalities.

She decided to go downstairs, have a cup of coffee, and read the paper until the girls woke up.

An hour and a half later, the girls both stomped downstairs, yawning. "Good morning, Aunt Sarah," Jessica said.

"Good morning, ladies," Sarah greeted with a smile. "What would the two of you like to do today?"

"I'm hungry," Rebecca said, eyes barely open and scratching her wild hair.

Jessica simply nodded in agreement.

"Tell you what, why don't you two get dressed and ready for the day. Then I will take us all out to breakfast. We can talk about what we will do while we eat. Sound good?"

"Yes," Jessica said.

Rebecca nodded as she yawned again. The two turned back around and stomped up the stairs.

After breakfast, they decided to go shopping. Sarah felt the urge to spoil her nieces to rid herself of the guilt of not seeing them often enough. They went to a bookstore. They each purchased at least five books each. She was happy to discover her nieces were avid readers. Then, they went to a few shopping boutiques along the pier. The twins saw matching dresses; of course, one was pink while the other was blue. They begged Sarah to get it for them. She finally agreed, stating they could wear it to church the next day. The girls looked disappointed that they still had to attend church even though their parents were out of town. They groaned but agreed.

Soon, they were hungry again, so they stopped at a burger stand along the pier. "Do you want to go to the movies after this?" Sarah asked.

They were sitting at a wooden picnic table facing the ocean in front of the burger stand. Jessica squished up her nose and shook her head. Rebecca shook her head shortly after Jessica.

Rebecca admitted, "I'm tired. Can we go back to your house? I wanna start reading one of my books." There was a sparkle in her brown eyes.

Sarah smiled proudly. "Absolutely. Sounds like a great idea to me. I'd like to start reading one of mine too." She rarely had time to read for pleasure since she was promoted to VP over five years ago. She thought back for a moment. In fact, this was the first full weekend she had taken off in the same amount of time. She thought of Claire momentarily, wondering if maybe her assistant was right. She may need to lighten up a bit and have some fun.

Sunday morning required much coaxing and bribing to get the girls dressed and ready to go to nine o'clock mass. She pulled up in her Mercedes just a few minutes before nine. Saint Michael's parking lot was nearly full, so she was lucky to find a parking spot near one of the exits. "Let's go, ladies," Sarah said.

Sarah was wearing black slacks, black pumps, and a white shirt that fit well. Her chestnut hair was down and pressed straight, falling to the middle of her back. She wore minimal makeup: mascara and lip gloss. She held each of the girls' hands as they walked to the church entrance. They scooted into the second-to-last pew, knelt to say a short prayer, and rose just as the procession began.

During the first reading, Sarah glanced around the church out of habit. When it was time to rise to their feet, her eyes landed upon the rear end of the man in the next pew directly in front of her. Her lip s

curled up a bit to a little devious smile.
Wow! What a perfect butt! She thought.
She immediately placed her hands to her
cheeks, embarrassed by the thought. She
was in church, for crying out loud! She tilted
her head and observed the rest of the man.
He had a small waist that expanded to a V
as her eyes roamed all the way up to his
shoulders. His shoulders were broad. His
hair was light brown and curly at the top
but trimmed on the sides. He was several
inches shorter than she was. Sarah tilted
her head again, and a sly smile appeared on
her lips. *I could wrap my legs around him
and swallow him up.* Her eyes widened.
What was wrong with her? Why was she
having these thoughts during mass? And for
a complete stranger? She said a tiny prayer,
*God, please forgive me. Don't strike me
down with lightning or anything... please.*

"Aunt Sarah," Jessica whispered,
tugging on her left hand. "Are you okay?"

Sarah simply nodded.

"Are you sure?" Rebecca asked to the
right of her."

Sarah nodded again.

"You have a little bit of sweat on your
forehead," Rebecca said.

The mass continued. When it was time to shake hands with church-goers around them as a sign of peace, the man she'd been drooling over turned around and made direct eye contact with Sarah. She blinked when she realized it was Jeremy Buchanan.

"Oh, hello," Jeremy said with a smile. He outstretched his right hand to shake Sarah's. "Peace be with you," he said as their hands touched.

As Sarah's hand touched his, she felt sparks ignite inside her. It was something she'd never felt before. Her stomach immediately reacted by flipping around, doing summersaults rapidly. Her throat felt strangely overly watered and then completely dry. She was barely able to say, "Peace be with you," back to him. He paused, and his lips curled into a smile. There was definitely a sparkle in his eyes. He finally let go of Sarah's hand and then offered his hand to each of the girls, taking turns to shake.

When Jeremy turned around, Sarah had to fan herself with one of the envelopes from the pew pockets. "Are you sure you're okay, Aunt Sarah?" Rebecca asked again.

"Because I have no problem with us leaving."

Sarah continued to fan herself and shook her head. Despite her hormonal panic attack in progress, her eyes wandered back over to Jeremy's derriere. *Talk about a piece of... Stop it!* She argued with herself. *Stop it now!* She forced her eyes to return to focus on the front of the church. She managed to go through the rest of the mass without gazing or drooling over Jeremy.

At the end of mass, as they were exiting the church, Jeremy waited by the massive brown door to the main entrance. Sarah and the girls each shook the priest's hand and then shuffled out. "Hi," Jeremy said, "Sarah, right?" He was in khaki pants and a light green polo shirt, which matched his eyes.

Her heart pitter-pattered. She cleared her throat and then offered a shaky smile. "Yes."

"I didn't know you went to this church. Do you live out here in Beach City?" Jeremy asked.

She nodded. "Yes, I moved here a couple of years ago and have been attending almost every Sunday since. I never noticed you here before, either."

"Stange, huh?"

She simply nodded, not knowing what else to say. She stood up straighter, and that old Amazon giant feeling came to her. She felt frustrated and inadequate inside. Why did she have to be cursed with the tall gene?

"Um," Jeremy bit the side of his mouth, then cleared his throat. He appeared a bit awkward and uncomfortable, shifting from side to side. *Get it together, man!* He shouted to himself. *I am a strong, confident, competent man! I can ask a beautiful woman out. I can do this... The worst thing that can happen is she says no... in front of two of my students... Uh, boy! Stop it! I am doing this. I am going for it. Sparks like that don't just happen for no reason!* "Um..." he repeated, shifting from foot to foot.

"Well," Sarah said. She took a deep breath in and a slow breath out. "I... I guess I will see you next Sunday then."

"Oh, um... actually..." he raised his right index finger. "I haven't eaten breakfast yet. Would you ladies like to go out for breakfast with me this morning? My treat."

Rebecca and Jessica eyed each other questioningly. Sarah's lips curled into a smile. "I'd love to. Girls, what do you think?"

"I'm always hungry," Rebecca said. "Sounds good to me."

"Okay," Jessica agreed.

Jeremy raised his eyebrows in pure surprise. "Really?"

Sarah laughed. "Sure, why not?"

In his mind, Jeremy was jumping up and down, pumping his fists in the air. He felt giddy inside.

"How about we meet you at The Yellow Waffle House on Main Street?" Sarah suggested.

"Okay, meet you there."

The Yellow Waffle House was predictably packed, but the hostess said they should be seated in approximately ten minutes. There was room for all four of them to sit on a long yellow cushioned bench inside the restaurant. "Do, did you girls do all of your homework?" Jeremy asked, wondering what else to talk about.

Rebecca rolled her eyes. "Really, Mr. Buchanan, that's all you got? I thought you'd have better moves than that."

Jeremy blushed.

Jessica elbowed her sister. "Don't be rude, Becky!" She leaned forward to see Jeremy's face. "Yes, Aunt Sarah made us do our homework as soon as we got to her house on Friday."

He cleared his throat. "So, are your parents on vacation this weekend?"

Sarah nodded for them. "Yes, they are partying it up in Vegas. They will be back later this evening."

"Well, that was nice of you to keep them," Jeremy said.

"Yep. Aunt Sarah is fun!" Jessica exclaimed.

Rebecca rolled her eyes.

Sarah wrapped an arm around Jessica and kissed the top of her head. It had been a long time since anyone labeled her as fun. She grinned at the compliment.

"See, there it is again," Jeremy said, pointing an index finger at her. "Your smile just lights up the place."

Rebecca stuck a finger in her mouth as if she were going to gag herself.

"Hey, do you like the 80's of something Rebecca?" Jeremy asked.

Rebecca shook her head and frowned from confusion.

"'Cause that was a total valley girl 80's move you did there," Jeremy explained with a chuckle.

"Oh, yeah, totally," Sarah added in a valley girl accent, "Like... Omigosh... totally for sure... gag me with a spoon... hit me with a pickup truck."

Jeremy and Jessica laughed, but Rebecca scowled and then said, "You guys are weird."

The hostess announced, "Jeremy, party of four." They all stood and then followed the waitress to the booth. The girls took one side, forcing Jeremy and Sarah to sit beside each other.

"Girls, are you okay with having breakfast with me? It must be weird to have breakfast with your teacher, right? You don't feel weird about it or anything, do you?"

Jessica shook her head to say no while Rebecca remained quiet and stared at him.

"Are you okay, Rebecca?" Sarah asked.

"Yes," she finally said but rolled her eyes for the umpteenth time.

"So, a bird told me since we are no longer allowed to have Christmas concerts or plays at our public school, we are going

61

to have a holiday school talent show," Jeremy said.

"Oh, how fun," Sarah said.

"I think it's lame that they won't let us have a Christmas play this year," Rebecca said. "I wanted to play Mary. I was so sure I would get the part."

Jessica nodded but said, "Well, we can do something together and enter the show."

Rebecca's mouth twisted to the side. "I guess so. What do you want to do?"

Just then, the waitress appeared. "Are you all ready to order, or do you need a little more time?"

"Oh, I already know what I want," Rebecca said, her tone completely changed to enthusiasm, "I want the colossal stack of waffles with strawberries and extra whipped cream and four extra-extra crispy bacon but not burnt. Oh… and a glass of milk when the waffles are ready but not before because the milk doesn't taste right if it's just sitting here while waiting for the waffles." The waitress looked like she wanted to say something but was biting her tongue. Instead, she nodded and scribbled Rebecca's order down.

Jessica said, "I'll have one waffle with blueberries and whipped cream, two slices of bacon, and orange juice. Thanks." The waitress smiled at Jessica and nodded.

"I'll have bacon and eggs with hash browns and wheat toast. Oh, and coffee, please."

Jeremy said, "I'll have what Becky is having." He pointed to Rebecca for the waitress' benefit. "Oh, but with coffee instead." He smiled. The waitress nodded, scribbled on her small notepad, and then grabbed the menus.

"We must all come here a lot because none of us even looked at the menus," Sarah said.

For the duration of breakfast, the topic of conversation was focused on the talent show. The twins dominated the conversation at the table, but Sarah welcomed the distraction as it eased the tension building inside herself. Throughout the breakfast, Sarah was conscious that her leg was constantly touching Jeremy's leg. Neither one of them moved away from the other even when they obviously could have.

At the end of the meal, they said goodbye to each other in the parking lot. I *want more!* Sarah thought as she and the girls walked to her Mercedes.

CHAPTER SIX

Claire was sitting in the breakroom sipping coffee and picking at a blueberry muffin when James and Roberta walked in. "So, how was your weekend, Claire?" James asked.

"You look kind of mopey," Roberta commented as she walked to the vending machine. She shoved a few quarters in and then selected powdered donuts. A few short seconds later, the machine spit the donuts out. Roberta grabbed the donuts and then wobbled to where Claire was sitting. She sat next to her.

"Big Carl and I had a fight. I don't know if we will make it much longer."

James snorted. "Well, at least it has been a record for you, right? You two have lasted more than a couple of weeks."

Claire nodded sadly. "I guess. I was just hoping he was THE ONE, you know? I know you both think I'm a slut, but really, I am just looking for my soul mate. I'm not going to settle for just anyone."

Roberta nodded in agreement. "I was very fortunate with my Lenny. We were high school sweethearts."

Claire gave Roberta a small smile. "How did you make it last for so long? You guys have been together for over thirty years, right?"

"Close to forty. We married when we were eighteen. No one could tell us we were too young." Roberta admitted, "But we were. I got pregnant right away. Had five kids. It wasn't easy. We had our storms." Roberta held her right hand out and started tallying with her fingers. "We went through jail time. I'm not saying which one of us went to jail. Bankruptcy. Miscarriage. Illnesses. I filed for divorce once, but a month later reconciled." She placed both hands on the table.

James sat motionless, staring at her. "Is any of that in your HR file?"

"It's none of the company's concern. It's all personal."

Claire took in a deep breath. "Oh, don't think I can do all that with one person."

"Oh, yes, you can. I'm not wishing it on anyone. When you love someone, you can take each other for granted. But when you go through the storms together, the way me and my Lenny did... the love grows."

"Really?" Claire asked doubtfully.

"Really. I mean... Lenny gets on my nerves. Don't get me wrong. It's part of his life's purpose to get on the only nerve I have left on a daily basis. Not to mention the man is super horny."

James covered his ears. "I don't want to hear this."

Roberta laughed and pulled his hands away from his ears.

"So, what did you argue about, anyway?" James asked.

"He doesn't want me to go to Texas for Thanksgiving. He wants me to meet his family," Claire said sadly.

"Oh, well, isn't that a good thing?" James asked.

"No, he's trying to take away my freedom. He's trying to forbid me from seeing my own family. That's not right."

"I agree, that isn't right. Why not compromise and tell Big Carl you will meet his family during Christmas?" Roberta suggested.

Claire nodded quietly.

"See. You two are in the transitional stage. Where all the fresh and new sparkly magic is starting to wear off a bit. But now, you are both moving toward the let's see how serious we are stage," Roberta explained.

Claire nodded.

Curiously, James asked, "So, after over thirty years, what stage are you and Lenny at?"

"Oh," Roberta said. She bit into a donut, chewed, and swallowed. "We are at the comfortable and settled phase. It's where you can fart during sex and laugh about it."

James laughed so hard that he started coughing.

Claire's eyes widened in horror and disbelief. "Omigosh! Did that really happen?"

Roberta started laughing. Her shoulders were shaking, and tears were forming from her eyes. "Yes," she said between giggles, "but you didn't hear it from me."

Sarah entered the breakroom with one of her enormous blueberry muffins. "What on earth are you all laughing and talking about? I could hear you all the way from the security desk."

None of them answered but instead continued the conversation.

"I would be totally devastated if that happened to me," Claire said, her hand over her heart.

When James finally stopped laughing, he asked Roberta," So what did you guys do after the gas passed?"

Roberta wiped her eyes with a napkin, still laughing a little. "Well, we just stopped what we were doing, then rolled over and laughed. It was kind of a moment killer, you know what I mean?"

Sarah felt out of place in the breakroom. She felt refreshed and happy when she first arrived at work, ready to tackle the work week. Sarah truly enjoyed her time with Jeremy, but now, she felt like an alien.

Claire finally addressed her, "Good morning, Sarah. Sorry for excluding you. I honestly don't think you want to hear the tales of Roberta Jenkins." She shook her head. "Trust me."

James let out a tiny laugh.

"Oh, guess who I ran into yesterday during mass?" Sarah asked Claire, completely changing the subject.

"Jesus," James joked.

Roberta shoved his shoulder. "Don't joke about Jesus."

Sarah ignored James and said to Sarah, "Your brother, Jeremy."

Claire's eyes lit up, and she sat straighter in her seat. "Really?"

"Yep, I had my nieces over the weekend, and when we went to mass yesterday, your brother was sitting in the pew in front of us. We even went out to breakfast after mass."

"Wow! That's great, Sarah!" Claire might have said a little too enthusiastically.

James' eyes narrowed, and suddenly, he became quiet.

The microwave beeped, and Sarah pulled out her muffin. "He's a very nice man, Claire. Thank you for introducing us," Sarah said, then walked out of the breakroom.

"Breakfast after mass doesn't count as a date, especially when her nieces were there too," James said.

Roberta nodded in agreement. "She has to say she went out on an actual date with them and that they kissed."

"Ah, man," Claire pouted.

"I was thinking... how will you get to Texas if you win? I doubt that you can get a flight out at the last minute," Roberta asked.

"Oh, no... I don't have to worry about it. My brother, Rick, has a private jet that he lets me and Jeremy use whenever we want," Claire said nonchalantly.

James blinked and was quiet for a moment. Finally, he said, "All this time you've known us, we could have been flying around?"

Claire shrugged her shoulders.

"Do you think he'd marry me? Does he have a taste for chocolate thunder?" James asked.

Claire rolled her eyes. "He's married. Knock it off," she said. Claire was feeling agitated. She really and truly wanted to go to Texas. Claire took a deep breath; her lips moved to the side, and she began to think. Only a few seconds later, Claire sprang to her feet and announced, "Oh, no! I forgot my phone in my car." She rushed out of the breakroom before anyone could stop her, then to her desk, unlocked her drawer, and quickly whipped out her purse. Claire shuffled through until she found her car keys. Then she rushed to the parking lot and glanced around to see if anyone was looking. When Claire saw the coast was clear, she unlocked her car. She turned on the light above the driver's seat and the headlights. Claire said a tiny prayer for yet more forgiveness for her deception. She rationalized, though, that it was for the sake of love... and so that she could go to Texas to see family she hadn't seen in years.

She then went back into the building and worked.

Claire hoped her car battery would be drained when her shift ended. When it was time to leave, she sat in her car, counted to three, and attempted to start it. The lights flashed for a moment and then clicked off. "Yes!" she shouted victoriously.

Claire grabbed her purse and headed back into the office. She replayed last week's performance: "Oh, no! I can't believe it! I left my headlights on, and now my battery is dead!" Claire whined loud enough for Sarah to hear from her office.

Claire called Jeremy using her cell phone. As soon as he picked up, she said, "Jeremy, you're not going to believe this, but my car battery died. Can you come over to my job and give me a jumpstart?"

She heard Jeremy sigh. "Really? Your battery died?"

"Yes," Claire said.

"Did you leave your headlights on on purpose?"

"Now, why would I want to do that?"

"Because you're you," he replied matter-of-factly.

"I wouldn't do something like that on purpose, Jeremy. Please come help me. You promised Daddy."

She could almost see him roll his eyes and shake his head. She grinned wickedly.

"Fine. I will be there in thirty."

"Okay," Claire said, doing a little victory dance near her desk.

"Everything okay?" Sarah asked, standing in the doorway between her office and Claire's desk.

Startled, Claire jumped a bit and placed her right hand over her heart. "Um, yes," she said.

"Is your brother coming to help you?" Sarah asked

"Yes," Claire said.

"Okay, good. You can type up a few new memos again while you wait for him, right?

Claire sighed but said resignedly, "Yes, of course."

Jeremy had to admit that he hoped Claire would send her boss out again to give him the keys. He had been thinking about Sarah nonstop since they had breakfast together. He had obviously misread the woman from their first impression. She wasn't rigid at all. She was funny and obviously adored her nieces. He wondered why she gave off the stern, rigid vibe when they first met. He also wondered if she would agree to go out on a date with him.

When he pulled into the parking lot, Claire and Sarah were waiting near Claire's car. Conveniently, the parking space next to her car was vacant. He parked his black Volkswagen Beetle next to her car. He smiled as he got out of his car.

Sarah smiled. "Hi, Jeremy," she said.

"Hi, Sarah, how are you?" he asked.

"I'm doing well, thanks."

Hmmm… Claire thought. *It's almost as if I'm not even here.* She grinned. *Looks like I'm going to Texas.*

"Do you have jumper cables, Claire?" Jeremy asked abruptly, startling Claire so much that she jumped.

She put her right hand over her heart. "Um," she thought for a moment. "Yes, I do. I think Dad put them in the emergency box he gave me the last time he visited."

"Sound like Dad," Jeremy said. He followed Claire to the back of her car. She popped the trunk and pulled out a medium-sized plastic tub container. Sure enough, there were jumper cables, first aid supplies, and a flashlight.

Jeremy grabbed the jumper cables and set to work on jumpstarting her car. "You need to let your car run for about twenty to thirty minutes."

Claire nodded. She looked around the lot and noticed that Sarah had vanished. She must have snuck away while Jeremy was bossing her around or, rather, instructing her on when to try starting her car. *Well, drat! That was just a waste of time! Ugh!*

CHAPTER SEVEN

On Tuesday, Sarah received another call from her sister-in-law asking if she would please pick the girls up from school again. "I hope this isn't going to be a habit, Kim. I can't just up and leave whenever I want to. I have meetings to attend and reports to review."

Sarah thought she heard sniffling. "I know, Sarah. I am sorry. I'm going through a lot right now, and I wouldn't ask if it weren't necessary."

"Where are you?" Sarah asked.

"I'm in Fresno again."

"How often do you have to go to Fresno?" Sarah asked.

"For the next few months, I will have to come out at least once a week."

"So, let's work together. The girls can spend the night with me instead of your neighbors. I can work from home on the days you need to travel. That way, no one is interrupted. I can take them to school and pick them up, okay? But you need to give me at least 48 hours' notice so I can plan it all out, okay?" Sarah offered.

She thought she heard her sister-in-law sniffling again.

"Is everything okay, Kim?" Sarah asked worriedly.

"Yes." Sniff, sniff. "Just stressed."

"Trying to be super mom, super wife, and magnificent hotel chain manager?"

Kim sighed a heavy sigh.

"Maybe you should consider staying home, Kim."

Now, she heard a gasp. Sarah assumed it was a gasp of disbelief. "I can't believe what I'm hearing... especially from you, of all people! You think I should just quit and throw away all that I've worked my butt off for all these years. The pain, the sacrifices, sweat, and tears... and you just want me to walk away?!"

"But, don't you see? That's the problem. The pain, the sacrifice, sweat, and tears... where is love and time for your family?"

"This coming from Miss High and Mighty VP, who rarely sees her family unless someone begs?" Kim said, exasperated.

Ouch, Sarah sighed. That stung a bit. Maybe she shouldn't have said anything. But, since she started it, she might as well explain what she meant. "Kim, I'm sorry. I didn't mean to insult you. If anything, I admire you. I mean... I am not married; I am not a parent of one kid, let alone two... I have a full schedule and lots of stress, and it's only me. How do you do it all without killing yourself? Yes, be proud of all you accomplished, but maybe it's time to walk away and enjoy your kids before they grow up and have their own lives."

"Easier said than done," Kim said, barely audible.

"Well, then, I can't believe I am about to say this... let me watch the girls more often. Not just when you need to go to Fresno. At least that way, it will lift some of your load. Plus, I do need to spend more time with them."

Kim sighed with relief, "Really, Sarah? Do you mean it?"

"Absolutely. But, as I said before, give me at least 48 hours' notice if you can."

"Oh..." Kim said, her voice shaky. "Thank you so much, Sarah. You don't know how much this means to me."

Sarah's eyes misted a bit. "No problem." She had much fun with the girls the previous weekend and looked forward to seeing them today.

Ten minutes later, she informed Claire she could leave for the day as soon as her work was done and explained she was leaving to pick up the girls and then work from home the remainder of the day.

When Sarah arrived at Beach City Elementary, she immediately noticed Jeremy directing parents and students into the parking lot. She had parked her car on the street near the school to avoid the traffic in the lot. She walked in her new black leather boots, black mini skirt, and Victoria's red form-fitting top.

Jeremy was talking to one of the moms as she approached. "We can discuss it over dinner tomorrow night if you'd like. I make a mean spaghetti and meatballs... some red wine and garlic bread... what do you say?"

Sarah felt her face get ho and her hands balled into fists. She slowed her approach to hear what Jeremy would say to the little gorgeous curly brunette with busts bursting out of her tight top. Jeremy shifted from foot to foot. He appeared nervous as he rubbed the back of his neck with his right hand. "Um... Ms. Jenkins, as I said to many of the other moms, it's against school policy to date the parents of students who attend school here. It's a conflict of interest."

Sarah bit her lip. She could tell he was lying. He was blinking his eyes rapidly, shifting from foot to foot and rubbing the back of his neck profusely. Not to mention that his eyes were roaming all over the place, except for Ms. Jenkins. Sarah smiled as she continued to walk towards him. *That's my man.* She stopped in her tracks and wondered where in the world that thought came from. She felt a slight surge of panic rush through her.

"Aunt Sarah?" Rebecca rushed up to her and bombarded her with an enormous hug.

"Yay! You're picking us up today?" Jessica shouted as she ran toward Sarah, her pink backpack over her shoulders. As soon as Rebecca was done hugging her, Jessica embraced her.

Jeremy turned to make eye contact with Sarah.

Damn! She's hot! Jeremy shouted in his head. He was surrounded by women daily, but ever since meeting her, she was the only one who clouded his mind with erotic images and longing. Seeing her, in reality, two days in a row and in red, his favorite color... and in what he guessed was Victoria's Secret top... *Woe! Down boy...* he told himself, *get ahold of yourself.*

He cleared his throat before approaching her with his hands on his hips, hoping he appeared manly and confident. "Two days in a row, huh?"

She smiled. Jeremy's heart sped up a bit.

"Yes, you would think the universe was trying to pull the two of us together or something, huh?" Sarah said. *Really? Did I say that out loud?* Mental forehead smack.

Rebecca and Jessica eyed one another. Then, they both shrugged their shoulders.

"I'm starting to wonder," Jeremy said. He rubbed his chin with his right hand and glanced around the parking lot to see if anyone was in hearing range. "Um... would you like to go out to dinner tonight?"

Rebecca and Jessica raised their eyebrows. Sarah did the same but immediately said, "Sure."

"Really?" Jeremy asked, surprised.

"Sure," Sarah said again. "I have some work to finish, and I'm sure the girls 'demanding, hard-nosed teacher assigned them gobs and gobs of homework... so it would have to be around seven," she teased.

He smiled. "Hey, we are preparing them for their future. The more homework, the better."

Both Rebecca and Jessica rolled their eyes.

"So, where should we meet?" Sarah asked.

"How about Paul's Italian Pizzeria?"

"Oh, cool! They have the best pizza!" Rebecca said.

"Pizza again?" Jessica whined.

"You know, they don't only have pizza. They have lasagna, spaghetti, and a bunch of other pasta dishes to choose from."

Jessica shrugged her shoulders. "Well, okay. I guess I will get lasagna. Can we have garlic bread?"

"Well, duh, Jess. They automatically give you bread when you order one of the pasta dishes."

"Okay, cool. I'm in," Jessica said as if her decision made or broke the dinner plans.

Sarah smiled. "Well, I guess there you have it. We will see you at Paul's Italian Pizzaria at seven tonight."

When Sarah and the girls arrived at the restaurant promptly at seven, they found Jeremy sitting in a booth at a corner of the restaurant. He waved to get their attention. Once again, the girls scooted in on one side of the booth, forcing Sarah to slide in next to Jeremy. "I hope we didn't keep you waiting too long," Sarah said.

"Oh, no, you are right on time," Jeremy said.

There was already garlic bread and peppered olive oil in the middle of the table. "The waitress just delivered it… so it's still hot," he said with a smile to Jessica.

Both girls grinned. Each grabbed a garlic breadstick, ripped off a piece, and dipped it in oil. "Only one piece for now. You can have more after you eat the real food," Srah said.

"This is real food," Rebecca said.

Sarah squinted at Rebecca, who was glaring at her with a warning. "You know exactly what I mean."

"Okaaaaay… Geesh!" Rebecca said but continued eating the garlic bread. The waitress arrived, and they each placed their orders. Rebecca ordered an individual thin-crust chicken and garlic pizza. Jessica ordered lasagna with extra garlic bread.

Jeremy and Sarah each ordered spaghetti with meatballs.

As the waitress walked away, Jeremy asked, "So, have you girls figured out what you will be doing for the talent show?"

Jessica shook her head.

"Hmmm," Sarah said. "Why not flashback to the eighties or early nineties? I can teach you a few dance moves."

Rebecca's mouth moved to the right side of her face as she contemplated the offer.

"Like what song? What dance?" Jessica asked.

"Something fun… maybe a Will Smith song or Run DMC…"

"How about *You Be Illin'* by Run DMC?" Jeremy suggested with a goofy grin.

Sarah laughed and then snorted. She covered her mouth.

"Did you just snort?" Jeremy asked with a laugh.

Sarah shook her head in denial.

"Yep, I'm pretty sure that was a snort, Aunt Sarah," Jessica said.

Rebecca shook her head in frustration. "No, I don't even know who or what you guys are talking about. I think Jessica and I will pick a current hit song that we like and know. But…" she shrugged her shoulders, "we can use some help coming up with a dance routine."

Sarah pouted but said, "Okay, deal."

"Hey, we can do a Doja Cat song," Jessica suggested excitedly.

Sarah blinked. "What's Doja Cat?"

Jeremy laughed. "It's not a what… She's a who… she's a female rap star."

"Oh," Sarah said.

Rebecca sighed, then offered, "When we get back to your house, I will let you listen to some of her songs on your phone."

Jessica reached across the table and placed a hand on Sarah's. She looked sympathetically at her aunt. "Aunt Sarah, you really need to let go of the eighties and nineties… they're dead."

Sarah's mouth dropped.

Jeremy burst out laughing; his shoulders shook, and he had to cover his mouth to silence himself. Just then, the waitress returned with their orders. The rest of the dinner was a combination of comfortable silence as they ate with momentary spurts of ideas for the talent show performance.

The rest of the week was filled with lots of work and excessive hours. Every year, it was expected to squeeze as many projects in as possible before the end of the year.

The group had decided to meet in the breakroom for lunch on Friday. James dragged himself into the room carrying a small brown bag containing his lunch. A moment later, Roberta joined, holding a plastic container full of leftover mashed potatoes and meatloaf. She immediately removed the lid and stuck it in the microwave.

Claire joined, carrying her own small brown paper bag. She sat down next to James. "Are you guys as tired as I am?"

"Yes, I can't wait for four o'clock to be here already."

"Me too," Roberta said with one hand on her hip. The microwave beeped, and she carefully pulled her food out.

James unfolded his lunch and opened it. He pulled out his tuna salad sandwich, then removed it from the plastic sandwich bag, and took a bite. He chewed and swallowed. "So, any progress report on your brother and Claire?"

Roberta joined Claire and James at the table. Claire shrugged sadly, then admitted, "No, not really."

Roberta tilted her head to the side as she fanned her lunch, hoping to cool it down. "Better get to steppin' on it.... It's thirteen days until Thanksgiving, so you have only twelve days to get them to go on a date and kiss," Roberta warned.

Claire's shoulders slumped, and she frowned. "Anyway, I can just talk you both into covering for me for the benefit. I already did most of the organizing. You would just need to show up at the Community Center and ensure everyone who said they'd deliver food would and that the tables are set up..."

James shook his head adamantly. "Nope, not doing it unless you win the bet."

Roberta kept quiet and began eating her food.

"Guess I won't see my parents and brothers this year," Claire mumbled sadly.

CHAPTER EIGHT

On Sunday morning, Sarah arrived at St. Michael's for nine o'clock mass. She wore black slacks, black flats, and a white button-down top. Her curly hair was hanging over one shoulder in a single neat braid. She took a seat four rows from the back of the main entrance. She knelt and made the sign of the cross. Just as she began praying, Jeremy scooted in next to her. He also knelt down and began to pray.

She couldn't help the small smile that crept up the corners of her mouth. *Thank you, Lord.* Then, she continued with her prayers.

After mass, Jeremy asked, "May I take you to breakfast?"

Sarah smiled. "Absolutely."

They agreed on The Yellow Waffle House again. They were seated at a table near a window overlooking the beach. The waitress quickly appeared to take their orders and soon left them alone. Sarah stared out the window, admiring the view of the waves crashing and a few surfers riding their boards in the distance. "It's beautiful, isn't it?" Jeremy asked.

Sarah nodded.

"So, what are your plans for Thanksgiving?" Jeremy asked.

"Oh, my brother and sister-in-law invited me over. I'm in charge of bringing the pies and ice cream. I can handle that," Sarah said with a smile.

"Not much of a cook?"

"Depends on my mood. If I'm in the mood, I can appear to be a gourmet chef, but if I'm not in the mood, which is most of the time… it's burnt or undercooked."

"I'll have to remember that." He said.

"What about you? What are your plans?"

"My sister is trying to convince me to go with her to Texas to see the rest of the family," Jeremy said casually. He shook his head as if he were conflicted.

Sarah frowned, confused. "Huh? She never mentioned she would be out of town."

"What do you mean?"

"Claire volunteered to be in charge of the Thanksgiving Benefit at the Community Center. Our company is the largest sponsor, but we get other businesses to either donate or cater the event. She's been handling it every year since she started working with me. Why didn't she say anything?" Claire asked.

Jeremy shook his head, "Hmmm... not sure. She sounds pretty confident that she's going. Are you sure she actually volunteered, or did someone just say she was handling it?"

Sarah thought for a moment. "Oh," she said in an almost inaudible tone. "Maybe I forced it on her just out of habit." She covered her mouth. "But still, why didn't she say anything? I could have found someone else, or I could have even handled it."

"Well, maybe you should talk to her about it tomorrow when you're back at work, Jeremy suggested.

"Yes, I will. Did Claire already buy her airline tickets?"

Just then, the waitress returned with their orders: blueberry pancakes with sausage for Sarah and colossal waffles with strawberries and extra whipped cream for Jeremy. Oh, and of course, four extra crispy strips of bacon for him as well.

When the waitress disappeared, Jeremy cleared his throat uncomfortably,

"Well, that's the frustrating thing about my perfect brothers. Not only are they both six foot two, but they are also extremely well off in the real estate business. One of them has a private jet ready for use by any family member at any time."

Sarah tilted her head. "You sound a tad bit bitter."

"Well, let's just say I'm the family's black sheep, but even more so since I supposedly dragged Claire with me here to California."

"Really?"

Jeremy licked his lips, took a bit of bacon, groaned from delight, then went back to scowling when he resumed talking about his family. "For whatever reason, the family seems to believe that Claire has worshiped the ground I've walked on since she was a baby. My mom says she worshiped me ever since she was in her womb, but... she is known to exaggerate. I know that none of it is true, considering we constantly argue. But she decided to go to college out here soon after I moved here. But that could be for the same reasons I left. I didn't want to be a real estate mogul. I didn't want to be competitive either. My dad was in real estate, but not the way my brothers are now. My dad did well enough to keep our family home and put us all through college."

Sarah took a bite of her blueberry waffles and nodded, encouraging him to continue talking.

He finally sliced his strawberry waffles and took a bite as well. When he was done chewing, he explained, "No one really supported my decision to pursue teaching elementary kids. They don't understand how great it feels to teach a kid something new and see the spark in their eyes when they catch on. I want to make a real difference, you know?"

Sarah nodded.

"So anyway, enough about me... what brought you to Beach City?"

She smiled and laughed a bit, "I guess Claire and I have much more in common than we realized. I followed my brother here. We've always lived in California but up north. When he told me he was moving here with his wife, I immediately started searching for internal jobs close to Beach City. I was a director at the San Francisco office... I saw the VP position open and took a long shot and applied."

"And, obviously, you won the position. What about your parents?" he asked before biting into another strip of bacon.

"They passed away over ten years ago," she explained. "Car accident."

"Oh, I'm sorry."

She nodded. "Anyway," she said, quickly changing the subject before she would see the predictable unwanted sympathy in Jeremy's eyes. "What are your plans for the rest of the day?"

"Actually," he said with a grin, "I was going to ask if you'd like to come with me to pick up my puppy after we eat."

She smiled wide, "Puppy? Really?"

"Yes," he explained, "I have been trying to adopt him for four weeks now. But I finally got approval, and they told me I could pick him up today."

"Why did it take so long?"

"Well, since all the animals are rescued, they want to make sure they go to homes that genuinely want them. They also want to ensure they are going to safe and loving homes. So, I had to have supervised visits with Buster. Then, they came by my condo to check it out. They wanted to see that I had enough space for him. If not, I could take him to a park close by instead. Then I got to keep him for a few days over a week ago, and I miss the little guy. But they called me yesterday and told me I was officially a daddy to a goofy Lab-German Shepherd mix. He's brown with pointy ears like a German Shepherd but a goofball like a Lab." Jeremy laughed.

"Well, yes, I'd love to meet Buster. Congratulations!" She held up her mug of coffee. He held his up, and then they clicked cups and sipped.

"Do you have any pets?" He asked.

She shook her head, "No, I always wanted either a cat, dog, or even a few fish, but I'm not home often enough, so it doesn't seem right to have a pet if I'm rarely there. You know?"

He nodded in understanding. "So, do you plan to always be a corporate lady, or do you ever see yourself as having a family?"

"Oh, I want it all." She shook her head and said, "It's ironic that I say that. Just last week, I was suggesting to my sister-in-law that she should consider becoming a full-time mom and quitting her job."

"And how did she take that?" Jeremy asked, taking another sip of his coffee.

"She almost bit my head off. Good thing it was over the phone. I don't know what she would have done to me if we were face to face."

"So you think she should stay at home, but you plan on having a family and working in the corporate world."

She frowned, then shrugged her shoulders. "I'm thirty-five. I can hear the alarms ringing. I had this huge plan to have an executive position, three kids, a cat, a dog, and a husband by the time I was thirty."

He stopped eating and then put his elbows on the table. "So, you hit one of the goals... what about the rest?"

"I'd like to say that age doesn't matter, but in reality, my eggs will shrivel up any day now."

He laughed.

She held a finger up, "Oh, and let me correct you... I actually did have a husband. But that was a huge mistake at the age of eighteen. The marriage lasted three months. We will leave that alone."

His mouth shifted to the side, but he said, "Thank you for your honesty. I might as well say I am thirty-three years old. Hope you don't mind dating someone younger than you... and shorter."

She felt shaky. Sarah's heart raced. She felt bubbly inside. "Um... dating... is this a date?" She asked.

Crap! Why did I have to go and say the four-letter word? Jeremy chastised himself. "Um..." he coughed. "Um... well... if you want to call it a date, I'll gladly call it a date." He rubbed the back of his neck nervously.

She smiled her beautiful, confident smile. "It's a date."

"Sooo... does that mean you are okay with me being younger and shorter than you? For some women, it's an issue," he said.

"Psst..." she waved her hand, "You're not that much younger than me. Give me a break," she took a bite of her sausage. As for height, as long as you're okay with dating a woman of Amazon proportions, then I am okay."

He laughed. "I guess everyone has their own hang-ups, right?"

"Right."

After eating, Claire left her car in the parking lot and slid into Jeremy's black Beetle. He drove to the Pet Rescue Clinic, which was just a ten-minute drive from the restaurant. The clinic was located on a few acres of property. There were enormous kennels with dogs, puppies, cats, kittens, and birds galore. There was a section where dogs a few dogs let loose to roam freely for a certain amount of time, then back into the kennels, rotating the dogs or puppies out.

Sarah followed Jeremy. He finally stopped in front of a kennel with the name "BUSTER" and a note saying, "Going home today."

"Buster!" Jeremy shouted in a booming and proud voice. "What's up, buddy? Are you ready to go home now?" Buster had been in a ball to the back of the kennel. But as soon as he heard Jeremy's voice, he sprung to his feet, rushed up to the kennel door, and barked a happy bark. He stuck his right paw up, waving. "Look at you! You remembered what I taught you, huh?" Jeremy reached into his pocket and handed Buster a little dog treat. "Good boy, let's get you home."

"Hi, Mr. Buchanan. " Sarah and Jeremy turned to the female voice behind them. It was a volunteer in jeans and a Pet Rescue Clinic t-shirt. I need you to sign a few forms, and then you can take him home."

"Okay," Jeremy said, disappointed. He couldn't wait to get the guy out of the kennel. After signing all the necessary paperwork and donating to the rescue clinic, Jeremy happily led Buster to his car with Sarah.

"He's a handsome fella! He's huge and adorable," Sarah admired the puppy as they walked to the car.

"He's got to grow into his paws. Buster will probably weigh about ninety pounds by the time he's done growing, and he'll probably be at least twice the size he is now," Jeremy said with pride.

At first, Buster sat in the back while Sarah sat in the passenger seat. But, as soon as the car was set into motion, Buster decided to squeeze between the driver and passenger seats and onto Sarah's lap. He gave Sarah a wet, slobbery kiss from her chin all the way up to her forehead. She laughed a heartfelt laugh. "Bleh," she giggled. "Puppy breath."

"Buster! Down! Get back there."

"No, he's fine. He's excited. It's his first day out of the kennel for good," she said.

"You sure you're okay? He's going to get hair all over your nice dress slacks and pretty much everywhere," Jeremy said, glancing at her and Buster as they waited at the traffic light.

"It's fine, really," she said, still laughing. "I can just wash it all when I get home."

"So, would you tag along with me to the pet store? I want a better collar, leash, water bowl, food bowl, and a doggy bed. Then we can take him to the dog park."

"Sure," Sarah agreed. She scratched Buster's back as he looked out the window and panted.

CHAPTER NINE

On Tuesday, Sarah sat in her office and daydreamed. She was supposed to be reviewing files on a few proposed new software apps being developed for current clients, but she could not focus. Sarah kept thinking of her Sunday with Jeremy. She hadn't had that much since... well... since... ever! It wasn't as if they even did anything spectacular. She had spent the entire day with Jeremy and Buster. Jeremy had held Sarah's hand the entire time they were at the dog park, except for when he had to run after Buster for one reason or another.

Just after two in the afternoon, Claire tapped on her already-opened door. "Um, Sarah?" Claire asked.

Sarah blinked and then glanced up from her computer screen. "Yes?"

"Everything okay?" Claire asked.

"Yes."

"Are you sure?" Claire asked doubtfully.

"Yes, why?" Sarah asked with a puzzled look on her face.

"Well, it's just that you haven't called me into your office at all today. You usually have me in your office at least ten times by now," Claire said matter-of-factly.

"Oh," Sarah tilted her head to the side. "I have had other stuff on my mind today, and honestly, I haven't accomplished much."

"Oh, okay. Well, just let me know if you need anything," Claire said worriedly, then slowly walked back to her desk.

At three o'clock, Jeremy called Claire on her cellphone. "Hey, Jer! What's up?" She asked.

"Um... this is going to sound weird, but can I talk to Sarah?" Jeremy asked in a low voice.

Claire smiled wide. "Absolutely," she said.

Claire tapped on Sarah's opened door again. Sarah had the same blank expression on her face as she had earlier. "Um, Sarah?"

"Yes?"

"Um... my brother wants to talk to you," Claire held up her cell phone and offered it to her.

"Oh, really?" Sarah almost squealed from surprise and delight.

"Yep," Claire answered, nudging the phone at her.

Sarah accepted the phone with perfectly manicured red painted nails. She had a tiny white flower painted on each of the ring fingers. She cleared her throat and then said, "Jeremy?"

"Hey Sarah, how are you?"

"I'm good, what about you?" Sarah asked.

"Pretty good. I meant to get your phone number on Sunday but got distracted by Buster. So, before we continue this conversation, what's your phone number? If you don't mind my asking," Jeremy said nervously but did his best to sound confident.

She smiled and then rattled off her cell phone number.

"So, what are you doing tonight?" Jeremy asked.

"Well, considering I've been daydreaming most of the day, I should continue working from home. But, honestly, my mind will not allow it.

"Great!" Jeremy said, then corrected himself, "It's great that you won't be working tonight. Would you like me to pick you up for dinner and a movie? A real date?"

Sarah's heart pitter-pattered nervously and wildly in her chest. She grinned. "Yes, that sounds great!"

"Okay, what's your address?"

She gave him the address and then asked, "What time?"

"How about six?" He suggested.

"Sure. Sounds great," Sarah said.

"Okay, see you then. Bye," Jeremy said, then disconnected right after Sarah said goodbye. Sarah clicked the end button on Claire's cell phone, bounced excitedly in her seat, and handed the phone back to Sarah.

Claire held her cell phone and glanced down at it. Looking back at her boss, Claire bit her lower lip. "What was that all about, out?"

"Your brother just asked me out on a date," Sarah announced, still grinning.

"Really?" Claire said, slightly shocked. She had thought she would need to do more damage to her own care at least one more time to get the two of them to notice each other.

"Yes. We actually had a date on Sunday. So this will be our second date."

"Really?" Claire asked, astonished. Her eyebrows lifted.

"Yes," Sarah said.

"So, did you guys kiss?" Claire asked, hopefully.

Sarah shook her head. Today, she wore her hair naturally curly. Each time she moved her head, curls bounced and hit her cheeks.

"Oh," Claire said disappointedly.

Jeremy and Sarah sat in a booth at Duke's Steak, Bar and Grill. There was hay on the concrete floor, and the tables were covered with red and white checked tablecloths. Six bottles of barbeque sauces were in a wire-carrying case in the center of the table. A waitress placed a basket of mini cornbread on the table and handed them the menus. The waitress was dressed in denim Daisy Duke shorts, a white button-up tank top, cowboy boots, and blond hair in pigtails. "I'll be right back to get your orders."

Sarah smirked. "Hmm… so do you come here often?"

"About once a month, why?" Jeremy asked.

"I could see how this place would appeal to men… that's all."

"Hey, it's a family restaurant," Jeremy said, then pointed to a young family with a toddler playing under the booth they were sitting at and an infant in a wooden high chair.

"Hmm… okay," Sarah mumbled.

She perused the menu.

"You seem a little on the edgy side tonight. Everything okay?" Jeremy asked.

She glanced at him and said, "Honestly, I've been completely out of sorts since the moment we met."

He raised his eyebrows and then said, "Really?"

"Yes."

"Is that a good thing or a bad thing?"

"It's too soon to tell," she admitted. "I can't focus on work ever since I spent the day on Sunday, which is not good from a work perspective. I've got tons of reports to go over and tons of apps to review and approve or disapprove. So many projects are trying to be pushed in before the end of the year, and I need to read and review every single detail, but I just don't want to. It's not good. I've worked so hard to get to where I am, and I have to work twice as hard to stay where I am."

"Oh," he said sadly, "I'm sorry. If you didn't want to go to dinner, we could have postponed it until all your work is done."

She shook her head. "See... that's just it. There's never no work to be done. It's a constant stream. It's all urgent, and it's even more at the end of the year."

"Oh," he said softly, unsure what else to say. He frowned, then resumed glancing at the menu.

"I'm sorry. I shouldn't have said anything. Let's figure out what to eat and enjoy our time together."

Kind of hard to enjoy now that I feel like a burden, Jeremy thought. Now, he felt agitated but did his best to hide it.

They were quiet until the waitress returned a few minutes later. Sarah ordered Filet Minot with spicy potato wedges and corn on the cob. In contrast, Jeremy ordered barbeque chicken breasts, a slab of baby back ribs, a stuffed loaded baked potato, and coleslaw. He ordered a beer while Sarah ordered a glass of merlot.

"So, how is Buster?" Sarah asked, hoping to change the mood.

The question brought a smile to Jeremy's face. "It's like raising a kid. He is obsessed with squirrels, lizards, and anything that flies. I don't have a big backyard, but it's big enough to have any one of those visitors, and he goes completely berserk. He hops around chasing after whatever moves. He is still getting down his paw and eye coordination, so he often slips and slides or runs into things. I am pretty sure he smiles at me in the morning and when I get home."

Sarah laughed and smiled. She noticed a sparkle in his eyes when he talked about his puppy—the same sparkle she daydreamed about constantly.

"So, have you decided if you're going to Texas for Thanksgiving?"

"Yes, I told my brothers I'd be there Wednesday night. I'm leaving right after school lets out. We close at noon that day."

"I meant to talk to Sarah about the benefit, but I kept getting distracted or, in general, dreamland, so I haven't gotten around to it. There is no need for her to feel obligated to run the benefit. In fact, I'll send her a text now so I don't forget." She reached into her purse and pulled out her cell phone. She searched for Sarah's number and then sent her a text:

ND 2 TLK 2 U RE Benefit 2moro

Then clicked send.

Their food soon arrived. In between bites, they chit-chatted about the upcoming talent show, more about Buster, movies, and books.

Jeremy held Sarah's hand as they walked out of the restaurant and to the parking lot. Sarah sighed a heavy sigh.

"Uh, oh," Jeremy sighed, too. "That sigh doesn't sound like it's a good thing."

Sarah stomped her stiletto. He looked up at her. She made a pouting, whining face. "You know... I think you hang out with my sister a little too much because you totally made the foot stomp and face that she does when she has to do something she really doesn't want to do."

Despite herself, she laughed but then tilted her head from exasperation. "I'm just getting on my own nerves. Sorry. I won't be able to do the movies tonight. I just have so much to catch up on today. It's going to be a long night of coffee and reports. Then I'll have to try to regain focus early in the morning."

Jeremy stuck his hands in his pockets, leaned back on his heels, and bounced back on his toes. "So, I guess there are no dates for you on school nights?" he asked.

She smiled sadly and nodded. "At least not until the end of the year, when the madness is over. I'm sorry."

He raised his hands up, "No, no… no more apologizing. I understand. I look forward to the weekends, and if all else fails, I'll see you at church, right?"

"Right," she agreed.

They walked to his black Beetle, and then he took her home. He walked her to her door, waited until she unlocked the front door, and went inside. Oh, how he wanted to kiss her and more, but she obviously wanted to get inside and work. *Bummer,* he thought.

CHAPTER TEN

Claire slid into her chair at her desk on Thursday with a smile. She was happy until Sarah stomped past her desk two minutes later with red eyes and a scowl. "Uh, boy," Claire mumbled under her breath.

"Claire..." Sarah called out from her office. "Do I have any eye drops?"

"Yes, it's in your middle drawer to the right, next to your other compact mirror case."

"Okay, thank you," Sarah said.

A few seconds later, she said, "Claire... coffee... please... better yet, mind going to the coffee shop down the street? My treat. Get whatever you want."

Claire perked up at the thought of free gourmet coffee and a chance to leave the office. She scooted out of her chair, grabbed her purse and car keys, and entered Sarah's office. She stuck her right hand out.

Claire slapped a couple of twenties in her hand. "You can take the break room crew with you." Sarah slipped off her heels and stuck them under her desk. "I'll be doing triple work today, so I apologize ahead of time for any attitude I may swing your way."

Claire blinked, surprised. She'd never offered to buy gourmet coffee for herself and her friends, much less apologize ahead of time for her moodiness. She couldn't help herself; she asked, "So, how did the date with my brother go?"

Sarah took a deep breath in and slowly let it out. She closed her eyes for a moment and then opened them to look Claire in the eyes. "I would love to spend more time with your brother, but you know how it gets here at the end of the year—total chaos. I just don't think I can take a relationship right now."

"Oh," Claire said sadly.

"Geesh, you sound so much like your brother," Sarah said sadly and tiredly.

"So, did you kiss yet?" Claire asked, hopefully.

Sarah shook her head.

Claire pouted.

"Oh, but before I forget, I've been wanting to talk to you about the benefit," Sarah said, rubbing her feet under her desk. "Go to Texas. You don't have to worry about the benefit."

Claire's mouth dropped open from disbelief and surprise. "I don't."

"Of course not. Promise me that next time you don't want to do something, you will speak up, though. I had no idea you had other plans. I just assumed you wanted to do it."

"Oh, okay," Claire said.

"Besides, James should be running it. He'll pick up where you left off," Sarah said.

Claire snorted.

"Well, when you go to the coffee shop, can you get me one of those espresso brownies too?"

"Okay," Claire said. "And you want a large white mocha, right?"

"Yes, please."

"Okay."

Claire stopped at Roberta's and James's desks on her way out. They all ran out of the building before Sarah changed her mind. They placed their orders and then took a seat at one of the small round tables in the café. Claire informed them what Sarah had said regarding the benefit. Roberta laughed while James gasped loudly, then slapped the table in protest, causing other patrons to turn and start at the group. "Well, don't think that the bet is off just because our boss excused you from the benefit," he warned.

"What do you mean?" Claire asked.

"Well," James said, moving his head from side to side as he said each word, "if those two don't kiss, you are still washing my car, doing my laundry, my housework, and mowing my lawn for a month."

"What??" Claire said, shoving his shoulder. "That wasn't part of the bet."

"Well, now that I'm forced to deal with this benefit, it is... if they don't kiss."

Roberta laughed.

On Friday evening, Jeremy called Sarah. Sarah avoided his calls and let them go to voice mail. She did the same when he called on Saturday. On Sunday, he sat next to her and held her hand during much of the mass, but afterward, she made up an excuse about work and left soon after church.

Jeremy felt deflated and rejected. On Monday, he agreed when Leslie Jenkins once again asked if he'd like to go out for dinner and a movie. Surprising himself and her. When the time came to meet Leslie at Paul's Italian Pizzeria, he felt like a scoundrel. Jeremy felt as if he were betraying Sarah. His heart squeezed in his chest. He missed her. He wanted to spend more time with her. Why was she pushing him away?

Leslie was already sitting in a booth and had waved him over. "Thanks for meeting me for dinner, Mr. Buchanan."

"You can call me Jeremy when we aren't at school, Leslie," he offered with a smile that didn't quite reach his eyes.

"Oh, okay," she said. "Thank you for meeting me, Jeremy."

You're welcome."

"I haven't gone on a date since I separated. It's been so crazy and stressful."

Jeremy only nodded.

"So, tell me... do you date often?" she asked.

"No, not really," he said.

"Anyone special?" Leslie asked cautiously.

Jeremy swallowed, dropped his head, and then scratched the back of his neck. He sighed. "Yes and no. I am in the process of falling hard for someone, but she'd been avoiding me for the past few days. I don't know what to do."

"Oh," Leslie said quietly.

"I'm sorry. This was a bad idea."

Leslie held her hands up. Her face flushed. "No, don't apologize. You have been trying to push me away for weeks, but I keep putting my claws into you. My mama is right. A guy just talks to me or is nice to me, and I cling to them like glue. How about we just have dinner together as friends? Does that sound good? This is NOT a date."

He smiled and nodded in agreement. The evening went along smoothly, with no stress and easy, light conversation. Just as they were leaving, Sarah walked in with her nieces. Sarah and the twins stood in the waiting area of the Pizzeria. When their eyes landed on Jeremy and Leslie, Sarah's nostrils flared while the twins glared at him.

Jeremy was flustered and confused. "Sarah," he sputtered, "it's so good to see you... I... I..."

Sarah stood up straighter in her UGG boots, jeans, and magenta sweatshirt. She clenched her teeth, and her jaw twitched. Jeremy was certain that if she had the ability to set fire with her eyes, he would have been nothing but simmering ashes at that moment. She narrowed her eyes at him. "You... you are obviously on a date. At least now I know I was nothing special. Good night."

Jessica and Rebecca continued to glare at him.

"Come on, girls. Let's pick up the pizzas and go home." The girls followed her to the register.

Leslie raised her eyebrows as she watched the other three females stomp off. "Ummm…" she said as she turned to Jeremy. "Do you want me to go talk to her? I can explain…"

It was Jeremy's turn to flare his nostrils. His hands were on his hips, and his eyes did not pull away from Sarah's perfectly behind. His temper skyrocketed to proportions he never thought possible. He held up his right hand, "No, I will straighten this out with her right now."

Leslie bit her lower lip, and her eyes widened. She mumbled, "Oh, I have to stay and watch this." Her eyes followed Jeremy as he followed them.

Jeremy tapped Sarah on her right shoulder. She was towering over him when she turned around, even without heels. He tilted his head back and puffed out his chest. "What do you think I was going to do, Sarah? Huh? Do you expect me to mope around all week-long pining and whing over you?" He tapped himself in the chest and said, "I'm a man, Sarah Alexander! I may be short. I may have a soft spot for dogs and cater to my little sister, but I'm a man. When I know I want something, I go after it. I want you, Sarah. I want you bad. I haven't pretended not to. But you've been pushing me away. So, what am I supposed to do? Not to mention the fact that this wasn't even a date. Oh, yes, I admit it. At first, it was intended to be one, but I regretted it as soon as I got here. I wanted to be on a date with you, but you are too busy for me. So, what am I supposed to do? I want to say again, this was not a date."

Sarah swallowed. She stared at him, absorbing his angry words, which he sputtered out so loudly and rapidly. The entire restaurant was staring at them.

Jeremy didn't care. He stood in his Nike tennis shoes on tippy toes, grabbed Sarah's cheek with both hands and kissed her senselessly. The kiss started off rough because Jeremy was, let's face it, feeling a tad bit passionate. He'd been dying to kiss her from the day they met in the parking lot. At first, she resisted. She had even tried to push him away, but he clung to her. Her lips softened, then parted, allowing him to use his tongue to explore hers. She wrapped her arms around his neck and bent down to kiss him back deeply.

"Really?" Rebecca said.

"Um… everyone is looking at us," Jessica said.

"No, they are looking at these two sucking faces! Gees, can you guys stop already?"

But they kept kissing until the cashier returned with the pizzas she had ordered. Claire cleared her throat, adjusted her sweatshirt, and paid for her order. She handed the pizza boxes to the girls and turned to Jeremy. "So… um…" she put her right hand to her swollen lips and asked in a high-pitched voice with wide eyes, "Do you want to join us for pizza?"

Jeremy looked up at her with victory and defiance in his eyes. "Nope. Here's what I am offering. I am going to Texas on Wednesday. While I am away, you think about me and that kiss. You think about whether or not you want to spend more time with me. If you want more kisses and maybe more than kisses. Think about what exactly you want and what's truly important. You can call me anytime. Then, the ball is in your court on the Monday after Thanksgiving weekend, Sarah. I want you and more, but I am not begging." Then he walked out with his chest puffed out and his head up high.

"Way to go, Mr. Buchanan!" Rebecca cheered, while Jessica appeared just as dumbfounded as Sarah.

CHAPTER ELEVEN

On Tuesday morning, Claire skipped into the break room. She was beaming ear to eat. When she saw James, she announced, "Ha, ha… I won… I won; I won; I won!"

James narrowed his eyes at her. Roberta clapped. "Good for you, Sarah!"

Claire was still grinning and nodding. "My brother called me late last night. He was talking super-fast and was out of breath. He said he was on a date with someone else, but then they started talking and agreed it was a mistake. They decided to not call it a date and just be friends… so, anyway, while they were at the pizzeria, Sarah showed up…. Just as they were walking out, she got the wrong idea. She huffed and puffed, and you know… basically, just being moody Sarah… then he shocked her and said this whole speech and well… then… he kissed her… right there in the restaurant!"

James shook his head, then briefly hung it in defeat. "Well, I still think you should at least wash my car."

Claire patted him gently on the shoulder. "Oh, James, it's okay. Love always wins."

Roberta nodded in agreement while James rolled his eyes.

On Wednesday, Claire and Jeremy were picked up in a limo and taken to the Burbank airport, where their brother's private jet was waiting to whisk them away to their family in Texas.

Sarah moped on Thursday morning. It was Thanksgiving. She was supposed to be perky and thankful for everything in her life, but all she could do was miss Jeremy. She was angry with herself for feeling so attached to someone she barely knew. She'd never felt this attached to anyone before... not even her ex-husband. But that was no comparison. She'd been young and dumb. She just wanted a way to get out of her parent's house, and getting married sounded like the perfect plan. Now, she would do anything to be with her parents. The familiar ache in her heart and soul crept its way inside. Her eyes burned, and tears began to fall. What was wrong with her?

She didn't get attached to people. People sucked! People were mean, and the ones she loved always left. Her parents, her ex-husband. She'd never told anyone about his cheating on her only days after they married. It still stung.

Her sister-in-law called her a little after eleven that morning to find out when she planned to arrive at their house. "Um... I think I will be late. I want to help with the benefit this year at the community center."

"Oh... really?" her sister-in-law sounded shocked.

"Yes, it's time I helped out and not expect others to do it all. I'll be there for dessert.... Well... I'll be bringing the dessert."

"Okay, if you're sure it's what you want to do. But we could wait for you," Kim offered.

"Oh, no," Sarah said, waving her hand even though Kim couldn't see it. "Don't wait for me. You guys eat and be merry. I'll be there later tonight with dessert as promised."

"Okay," Kim said. "See you later."

At the recreation center, James walked around with a clipboard in his hand, a blue tooth in his ear, and barking orders at anyone who would listen. Roberta covered the long rectangular tables with plastic tablecloths, placemats, silverware, and napkins. Next, she placed small floral centerpieces donated by Sokie's Flower Shop.

"Well, it all looks lovely," Sarah complimented Roberta.

Roberta smiled proudly. "Thank you. My daughter and granddaughter will be here to help serve in a little while."

"Great, the more the merrier, right?"

"Right," James said sarcastically as he passed by commanding volunteers carrying a big container of candied yams.

Around one o'clock, people started showing up for meals. Sarah, Roberta, and ten other people stood behind the mounds of food and began serving. Roberta introduced Sarah to her daughter and granddaughter: "Sarah, this is my daughter, Leslie. Leslie, this is my boss's boss, Sarah Alexander."

Sarah covered her mouth from embarrassment. Her eyes widened. Leslie was the petite, tiny brunette with long, curly hair that had Sarah's blood boiling from pure jealousy only a few nights before.

"Oh, wow!" Leslie laughed. "We met the other night. Now that it was a show! Let me tell you, Mama!"

"Oh, no... please... no... don't," Sarah begged.

"What?" Roberta looked from Sarah to her daughter, then back to Sarah again. "You two know each other."

"Well... kind of... we met... once," Sarah half explained.

"Leslie stood beside Sarah for the rest of the afternoon, serving food.

The busy, helpful work soothed Sarah's jumbled nerves and soul. She felt lighter and happier.

Sarah arrived at her brother and sister-in-law's house a little after six. She had a shopping bag full of ice cream in one hand and pies in the other. Her brother, Cedrick, opened the door. His six-foot frame filled the doorway. His chocolate skin, big brown mischievous eyes, full lips, bald head, and arms stretched wide to greet her. She thought he wanted a hug, but he was swift and quick. He reached for the bags of junk food and then closed the door. She stood on the porch, eyes squinting at the door. She heard his loud and obnoxious laugh behind the door. "Thanks, sis. Happy Turkey Day, Turkey!" He shouted.

She then heard Kim chastising him and opened the door. "Come on in... you know your brother."

Sarah shook her head, "Why should I be surprised? He does this to me every single year, but yet... I am still surprised."

Rebecca and Jessica rushed up to Sarah, enveloping her in hugs and kisses. "Ahh... now that is how you greet someone you love," Sarah said with a smile.

"So, how did it go at the rec center?" Kim asked as she wandered to the kitchen.

Sarah followed. The kitchen was bright with recessed lighting, modern chrome appliances, granite countertops, and food on the center island. "It went great. Lots of people showed up, and we had more than enough food. There were still people coming and going when my shift was over."

Cedrick was standing in the corner, dishing an enormous piece of apple pie. He stuck it in the microwave for a few seconds, then plopped scoopfuls of vanilla bean and chocolate ice cream on top. "Babe, do we have antiacid?" he asked before taking a bite.

Kim nodded.

Then he scooped another scoop of vanilla bean ice cream and added it to the pile.

"Are you going to give me a hug, at least?" Sarah asked.

Cedrick took a bit of pie with some ice cream and then approached his sister. He put his bowl of dessert and spoon on the island's edge. He spread out his arms and then enveloped Sarah in a bear hug. She squeezed him tight. She felt her throat build up with pressure, and tears began to trickle down her cheeks. Her brother rocked her side to side and let her cry. He rubbed her back, squeezed her once more, and kissed her on the forehead. "Hey, hey… what's with the tears?" He asked.

He pushed her away at arm's length, his hands on her, and then looked her straight in the eyes, examining her.

She looked down and wiped the tears away. "I've been so emotional lately. I've got things all wrong."

Kim approached the two of them and started rubbing Sarah's back too. "What's going on?"

"Well," Sarah sniffed. "I met someone."

That made Cedrick smile. "Well… it's about time you give me some nieces and nephews."

Kim nudged Cedrick. "Stop it, Ced… don't you see she'd conflicted?"

"She's in love," Cedrick said simply.

"But I hardly know him."

"Well, you obviously want to get to know him better. So do it… get to know him. Marry him and have some babies."

She shook her head. "You make it sound so simple."

"That's because it is."

"But work…"

"Work is working… work doesn't care about you, Sarah. People care about you."

"But I have a responsibility, and I have so much…"

"Delegate it," Kim said. "I fell into the trap, Sarah. You witnessed it. We've all been broke, and we have all worked hard to get to where we are. We have this thing inside us where we fear losing everything we worked so hard for. But, here's the thing…. You could get laid off out of the blue… you could lose everything in a natural disaster. You can get hit by a bus crossing the street. You can slip in the shower and break your neck. What is important in life? What is THE most important thing in life?"

Sarah looked broken and stared at Kim and Cedrick. They weren't going to answer the question for her. She needed to respond, and she needed to say it out loud: "Love."

Cedrick and Kim nodded. Cedrick pulled his sister in for another brotherly bear hug. "Yep." He kissed her on the forehead again, then let her go. He grabbed his dessert bowl and then joined his daughters in the living room to watch them play video games.

CHAPTER TWELVE

On Monday morning, Claire skipped into the break room. She had a box of donuts to share with James and Roberta. They happily accepted. "So, how was Texas?" James asked before slowly biting into a jelly donut. As he chewed, he shoved the sunglasses he was wearing higher up his nose.

"Amazing! Guess who was sitting all dapper and hot when I got to the plane?"

"Who?"

"Big Carl!" Claire shouted excitedly. "He surprised me. He had talked to my brother one day while I was in the shower, and they plotted the whole thing out. Can you believe it?" She exaggeratedly waved her left and back and forth.

"What's with the rock?!" Roberta shouted as she jumped out of her seat and grabbed Claire's hand.

"Oh, that? We're engaged!" Claire announced in a high-pitched squealing voice excitedly. "Can you believe it? Eeeee...."

James covered his ears with his index fingers. "Gees, Claire... have some mercy.

I'm nursing a slight hangover over here," James said in a low voice.

"Oh… sorry. Well, that explains why you're wearing sunglasses today."

He nodded slowly, then sipped coffee on his vending machine, and then took another bite of the donut.

Just then, Sarah entered the breakroom holding a muffin. "Hey Sarah, would you like a donut? Claire brought them in," Roberta said.

Sarah glanced at her muffin, made a face, and approached the group sitting at the table. She glanced at the open box of fresh, warm donuts and drooled. "Yes, please."

Claire stood beside her and extended her left hand to move the donut box closer to Sarah. She deliberately kept moving her left hand in exaggerated showmanship.

Sarah grabbed Claire's hand with much more gusto than Roberta had. "Look at the size of that monstrosity!" Sarah's eyes nearly popped out of her head.

Claire jumped up and down excitedly.

"When did this happen? In Texas? Did Big Carl go with you to Texas?" Sarah asked.

Claire nodded excitedly. "He asked me yesterday during breakfast in front of the whole family. Can you believe it? He even went down on one knee."

Sarah's eyes misted. She was truly delighted for Claire. "That's great, Claire. Congratulations!"

"Thanks," she said. "Hey, what size ring do you wear?" Claire asked Sarah.

"Seven," Sarah answered automatically without a second thought.

Roberta eyed Claire suspiciously. James was still delicately sipping coffee and a bit pale, especially considering his dark complexion. "Uh oh... that donut was a mistake," James said. "I think I must go home for the rest of the day." Roberta held in a laugh. She wondered when James would learn to control his partying ways, especially the day before he needed to work.

James made a heaving noise and then sprang to his feet. He rushed out of the breakroom.

Claire continued to talk animatedly about her trip to Texas. A few minutes later, James returned, appearing less pale.

"You hurled?" Roberta asked.

James nodded.

"Feeling better?"

"Ask me in a few hours," James whispered.

"Go home, James," Sarah commanded.

"No," James said stubbornly. "I'm HR."

Roberta, Claire, and Sarah shook their heads.

"Well, I have a call to get to," Sarah announced. "Don't stay in here too long. We've got lots to do." She grabbed another donut with another napkin and then left the breakroom.

"So, why'd you ask her for her ring size?" Roberta asked as soon as the door closed.

"In case Jeremy wants to know," Claire said confidently.

"You think those two are going to get engaged?" James asked.

"Absolutely. I am willing to bet they will get engaged before Christmas," Claire said, grinning.

Roberta's mouth shifted to the side doubtfully. "I don't know. That might be a stretch. According to my daughter, Sarah has a jealous streak."

Claire waved her hand dismissively. "It's called love, Roberta. It's love."

"Well, I'm in... I don't think they'll get engaged that quickly. If they don't, you should finally wash my car and buy me lunch every day for a month," James challenged.

"And if I win?" Claire asked.

"I'll buy you lunch for a month and wash your rinky-dink car," James offered with a laugh. Then he placed both hands on his head and massaged his temples and forehead.

"Deal," Claire said. James and Claire shook hands.

On Monday at four, Sarah left her office without her laptop and locked her door. Claire reached for her purse and stared up at Sarah. "Um... Sarah?"

"Yes?" Sarah asked as she put her coat on.

"You forgot your laptop and business bag," Claire said worriedly.

"Oh, no, I didn't. That's why I locked my office up. No more working after hours."

Sarah's mouth fell open.

"You can close your mouth now. I just realized what's important and what I want. I'm going after Jeremy."

Claire smiled broadly and looped her arm around Sarah's as they walked toward the exit. "Sarah, it's time I ask you: What are your intentions with my older brother?"

Sarah laughed. "It's all good intentions, Claire."

When they were standing in the parking lot next to Sarah's silver Mercedes, Claire asked, "Can I ask you something personal?"

"Sure," Sarah said. "You always do anyway."

"Remember a few weeks ago, you said you were a one-night stand kind of woman? Is that true? Because my brother is so NOT a one-night kind of guy... he's like the Sam Smith song, you know?"

Sarah grimaced. "I was hoping you forgot me mentioning that," Sarah said regretfully.

"Nope," Claire said, tapping her right temple with her right index finger. "I keep it all up here. Organized thoughts... remember?"

Sarah nodded reluctantly. "Well, I have to be honest. I went through a slutty hormonal phase a few years ago that honestly lasted for about a year. But one day, I just felt empty and tired. I started going back to church, and I've been celibate ever since."

"Wow!" Claire shouted.

Sarah immediately covered Claire's mouth with her right hand. "Now, promise me this will stay between the two of us. I will share the information with Jeremy when the time is right. You do not talk about my personal life with anyone. And I mean, NO ONE. Especially not the breakroom crew."

Claire nodded in agreement. Sarah slowly removed her hand from Claire's mouth.

"Well, you have my blessing, Sarah," Claire said with a big smile.

"I.... what?" Sarah asked,

"Go get my brother," Claire said.

Sarah straightened up her coat and said, "I will. Thank you." Claire gave Sarah her brother's address.

At five thirty, Sarah was dressed in jeans, tennis shoes, and a long-sleeved T-shirt. She stood on Jeremy's porch and knocked on the wooden door. She could hear Buster's paws scraping as he ran to the door with exuberant glee. She could also hear his barking and scratching on the door. "Buster! Calm down," Jeremy shouted inside.

She smiled.

When he opened the door, Buster leaped for joy, bouncing up and down on Sarah's legs. He was trying to lick her face.

"Hey, who watched Buster while you were in Texas?" Sarah asked curiously as she entered his home.

Jeremy didn't resist her entry but explained. "My neighbor. He has a lab, and now they are buddies."

Jeremy closed the door. Sarah knelt on the living room floor, and Buster licked her face all over. She closed her eyes and laughed. "I hope you have a lot of soap and a washcloth I can use in a minute," she said, still laughing. Buster was still licking her excitedly.

"Bleh, puppy breath…" she laughed.

Finally, Buster calmed down and was distracted by a squeaky toy Jeremy squeezed and tossed into another room. Buster jovially ran after the toy. "Let me get that soap and washcloth for you." He disappeared for a moment and returned with a small bar of soap and a washcloth. He handed it to her and pointed down the hall. "The bathroom is down the hall and the first door on the right."

"Thanks," she said.

After washing up, Sarah stared at herself in the mirror. She arrived at Jeremy's home makeup-free. She noticed, though, that it was the first time in years that she was truly relaxed. "Wow," she whispered, except for the jumbled nerves bouncing around in her stomach from her nervousness and excitement.

"Everything okay in there?" Jeremy asked from the other side of the bathroom door.

"Um… yes…" Sarah said as she opened the door.

Jeremy was standing directly in front of her when she opened the door. His arms were stretched from one side of the door jam to the other. He didn't budge. Sarah moved closer. He looked up at her. She bent over a little bit, then kissed him. He groaned and kissed her back. They wrapped themselves in each other. He managed to untuck her shirt, and his hands were getting ready to explore her body, but she stopped him.

Her forehead leaned down against his. They were both breathing hard. "I don't want us to get carried away," she said. "We still barely know each other. Let's date and see where this takes us."

He inhaled deeply, then nodded in agreement as he slowly exhaled.

Buster clumsily charged towards them, running down the hall with his squeaky toy in his mouth. He dropped the toy in front of them and barked.

"Wanna take our puppy for a walk?" Sarah asked.

Our puppy? Did she really just call Buster our puppy? Jeremy wondered in amazement and amusement. He nodded. Jeremy grabbed his keys, Buster's leash, and Sarah's hand. They walked for nearly an hour. They talked about everything and anything.

When they finally returned to Jeremy's place, he asked, "So, you have time for a relationship now?"

Sarah nodded. "I had a long talk with my brother and sister-in-law. I figured out what's important. We have something here, and I want to explore it."

"Me too.

She followed Jeremy into his tiny kitchen. It had an old stove and oven; the countertops were white tiles. She loved it; it felt like home. Jeremy reached into his refrigerator and tossed two steaks on the countertop. He closed the fridge and reached up on his tippy toes to take down a metal bowl filled with potatoes. He handed her the potatoes. "You peel the potatoes, and I will marinate the steaks. You can oversee the mashed potatoes."

She smiled. "I can handle that."

"I hope so," he joked.

"We have ready-made salad in the refrigerator. We just need to rinse it off when we are ready to eat."

"Sounds good."

"Red or white?" Jeremy asked, referring to wine.

"Red, always red."

"I'll remember that." He said.

When they ate, Jeremy announced, "Okay, so I have a serious question to ask you..."

Uh, boy! Sarah thought. *What does he want to know? Did Claire tell him about my shady past?* "Okay. Ask."

"Will you be my date to the talent show?" He asked seriously.

She laughed, took a sip of wine, and then answered, "Absolutely. I wouldn't miss it for the world."

"Well, you have to go... I mean... your goddaughters are in the show... it's a must.... But will you be my date?" He asked.

She grinned. "Yes, I will be your date."

"Yes... " he said with a little whoop.

They saw each other nearly every day for the next three weeks. The Friday before winter break was scheduled to begin was the night of the talent show. Jeremy had invited his sister to the event, to which she, in turn, invited James and Big Carl. Roberta was already planning to attend since her granddaughter was performing. Sarah sat next to Roberta. "My granddaughter has been practicing every night for the past two weeks. This is going to be great. I miss the Christmas plays, but I still think this will be great."

Sarah nodded. She'd helped her nieces with their dance routine.

Promptly at seven, a tall, lanky woman dressed in black pants, flats, and a white button-up shirt with a thin black tie approached the mic on stage. Her long, straight black hair was slicked back into a ponytail. "Good evening, ladies and gentlemen. Welcome to Beach City Elementary School's annual talent show. For those of you who don't know me, I'm Diane Phillips, the school principal. We thank you for joining our students today as they show off their skills and talents. We want to encourage the arts, and this is one way to do just that. So, sit back and enjoy." There was some mild clapping from the audience.

The principal remained on stage. She put her head down and then snapped her fingers. Two students rushed to the stage carrying a black coat and draped it over her. Once those students disappeared, another student rushed to the stage, holding a black hat and sunglasses. She placed both on the principal. When the student was off the stage, Jeremy smoothly slid onto the stage, wearing the same attire as Diane. Immediately, the Blues Brother's *Everybody Needs Somebody to Love* blasted over the speakers. The crowd went wild as Jeremy and Diane lip-synced and danced precisely how Dan Aykroyd and John Baluchi performed it. Sarah was quite impressed. She laughed and cheered during the entire performance.

"Well, that'll be a tough act to follow," Roberta said.

Claire nodded. "My brother is awesome, isn't he?"

James rolled his eyes in the typical James fashion.

A few acts later, the twins lip-synced and danced to a Doja Cat song. Sarah was most certain the school bleeped out several words from the rap. Right after the twins performed, Roberta's granddaughter performed a dance routine to an Ariana Grande song. There were more performances to follow, including a few live singers. All in all, it was a fun night.

CHAPTER THIRTEEN

Jeremy invited Sarah to Big Carl's house for Christmas Eve. Carl only lived a few houses away from her brother, to Sarah's delight. This made it convenient in that she could visit her brother for a short time and then join Jeremy at Carl's house. While she was at her brother's house, she passed the girls gifts to them. "You can't open them until tomorrow," she teased. They were seated in the living room, where the seven-foot decorated Christmas tree was.

"Oh, come on, Aunt Sarah!" Rebecca whined, holding the gift. She was shaking it aggressively. "Don't you want to see our expressions when we open the present from our favorite aunty."

Cedrick scowled, "You've been hanging out with my sister too much because, no, you are starting to sound just like her."

"Oh, stop," Sarah said, nudging her brother on his knee. He was sitting on the leather couch while she was sitting close to him on the floor. Her back was resting against the couch.

"Please, Aunt Sarah, can we open them?" Jessica begged. She was kneeling in front of the tree, gently holding the box that was the same size as Rebecca's.

"Okay, I want to see you open them."

The girls immediately ripped off the snowman wrapping paper and squealed in delight. "American Me Dolls!"

Cedrick rolled his eyes and then shook his head.

"I'm so glad they are still into dolls," Sarah said.

Kim nodded, "Me too."

"Well, at least I have Rebecca. She loves sports," Cedrick said.

Rebecca let out a squeal of delight: "Look, Jessica! They look just like us! Look! Mine even has a mole by her left eye, like mine! Eeee!! This is great! Thank you, Aunty Sarah!"

Sarah smiled.

She visited for a couple more hours, and then at six, she let her family know she needed to walk to Carl's house. To her surprise, Kim, Cedrick, and the girls invited themselves to join her. "Oh, okay. I guess the more, the merrier, right?"

"Don't worry. I'll bring a couple bottles of wine as a bribe for entry," Cedrick offered. He then strolled over to his small wine refrigerator that was behind his mini bar near the living room. He grabbed a Merlot and a Chardonnay. "This should do it."

The family then walked a few houses over to Carl's house. Carl owned the biggest house on the street. It was massive and impressive. Sarah could easily visualize Claire raising a family here. She was truly happy for her. Sarah rang the bell and was immediately bombarded with hugs and kisses. A house full of people was putting it mildly. There was a woman with bright red hair who was a few inches shorter than Jeremy, with bright green eyes and an enormous smile. "Hi, you must be Sarah. So good to meet you! I'm Lorraine Buchanan! Jeremy's mom." She stretched out her arms and embraced her in a hug.

"I... Jeremy didn't... he... I..." Sarah felt overwhelmed.

"I'm sorry about this, Sarah," Claire said. I tried to stop them all, but they insisted on flying out to meet you."

"It's Christmas! We want to be with everyone," an older man with a deep, booming Southern accent said from the bottom of the elaborate spiral staircase. He was well above six feet. He had his arms outstretched and embraced Sarah with a bear hug. "I'm THE Mr. Buchanan, but most people call me Craig. I'm Jeremy's dad."

Sarah's heart was racing out of control. She hadn't expected this welcoming committee.

Jeremy tapped his dad on the shoulder. "Can I have my lady now?" Jeremy asked with a smile.

"Sure, son," Craig said. He released his embrace of Sarah.

Sarah turned to see where her brother and his family were. They had made themselves at home and were already introducing themselves to those gathered around them.

Jeremy whispered to Sarah, "I'm sorry. I didn't know they were coming. They just arrived today. My brother has this habit of showing up out of the blue sometimes… and sometimes… he brings the entire family with him."

"Oh, don't apologize. It's great that your family is able to do this, you know? So many people don't have family around and are not celebrating Christmas because they feel like they have nothing to celebrate."

"Is that the way it was for you?" Jeremy asked.

Sarah nodded. "Yes, but I was blind and stupid. I didn't see the family that was right in front of me. I'm not just talking about my brother, sister-in-law, and the girls. I'm talking about them." She pointed to Claire, James, and Roberta. They were sitting on a couch near the enormous Christmas tree, talking and laughing. James had a genuine smile on his face as he sipped Egg Nog.

"Oh, be careful of the Egg Nog. My dad made it. There's more alcohol than nog."

She laughed.

Claire soon announced it was time to play Pictionary. There were several groans, but the twins jumped up and down excitedly.

The evening zoomed by with lots of noise, laughter, games, chatter, and even dancing. Around nine o'clock, Jeremy approached Sarah. She was sitting in a corner, waiting for her turn to draw the picture for another round of Pictionary. He offered his hand. "Mind coming with me for a moment?" he asked.

She nodded, accepted his hand, then followed him. He skillfully maneuvered his way around the crowd of family, friends, and loved ones. He led them down a hall and to a door to the right. He opened the door and then led her inside. He locked the door, then flicked the light on. They were in a bathroom. And what a bathroom it was! It was huge with peach-colored tile, a jacuzzi tub, and a glass shower with many knobs, gadgets, and gizmos. There was a double sink and a space-age toilet. Sarah was still holding her glass of wine. She took a sip and then said, "Wow! This is a little much, don't you think?" Sarah asked.

"I'm glad you said that because I'd never be able to afford something like this."

"Oh, no… don't want it. This would stress me out. I love… I absolutely love… your house. It feels like home. Especially with Buster running around like a maniac."

He laughed and pulled her close. He took her wine glass and placed it on the sink. He kissed her. "Merry Christmas Eve."

"Merry Christmas Eve," she said back at him.

"I just needed a little time alone with you. I hope you don't mind," Jeremy said.

She kissed him again, but then Sarah felt a little weight on her chest. "You know… I have to come clean about something… I mean… it was a long, long time ago, but it was a period of time of bad decisions, and I think you should know..."

"Yeah, Claire already told me about your spinster days. It's okay. I wasn't a saint either. But we've been good for the past few years, right?"

Sarah's mouth dropped open. "She told you?"

"Psttt.... She probably told Roberta and James, too. You should know my sister can't keep a secret even if her life depended on it."

"I'll remember that," she said pointedly, then shook her head.

"And speaking of my sister... she mentioned you wear a size seven. Is that right?" he asked, then kissed her.

"What?" Sarah asked, utterly confused.

He dropped down to one knee and pulled out a blue velvet box. He swallowed. "I know we've only known each other for a few weeks, but I feel like I've known you my whole life. You were the missing chunk I've been searching for all my life. Sarah..." He popped open the box; inside was a simple engagement ring. Tears filled her eyes. "Will you marry me?" He asked. He held his breath. *Please say yes, please say yes. I'll die if she doesn't want to spend the rest of our lives together.*

She nodded and choked back tears. "Yes, Jeremy, oh, God, yes!" He immediately slipped the ring onto her finger and then jumped to his feet. They embraced each other in a tight hug. He kissed her over and over again.

"I love you, Sarah."

"I love you too, Jeremy."

They both held each other and cried happy tears.

There was an obnoxious knock on the door.

"What did she say?" Claire shouted.

"Yeah, bro, what'd she say?" A deep voice that sounded much like Cedrick asked.

They both laughed.

"Are you ready to face the crazy people beyond this door?" He asked.

She nodded with another laugh, "Yes."

"Okay, let's do this," Jeremy said. He grabbed Sarah's left hand. As soon as he opened the door, he lifted her left hand and shouted, "She said yes! Everybody, she said yes!"

There were whoops, laughter, cheers, and high-fives.

James dropped his head in defeat and shook his head.

"Yes!" Claire jumped up and down. "I won again!" Roberta gave her a high five.

www.ingramcontent.com/pod-product-compliance
Lightning Source LLC
Chambersburg PA
CBHW071347170626
46811CB00003B/1014